"Tonight, I found myself wishing you'd been beside me," Drew said softly.

Though his words sent a flood of heat flowing through her veins, Lori forced a light tone. "Only because you feel safe with me. You know I'm not out to get married."

Drew chuckled. "At least not to an older man with kids."

"True," Lori said. "But for an old guy, you can be lots of fun. Tonight, I found myself wishing I was with you, too."

"Which goes to prove we're still on the same wavelength. So, why didn't we go together?"

"You didn't ask," Lori said softly.

He moved closer and tilted her face up with his fingers. "I'm asking now. Will you go out with me Friday night?"

His closeness made her voice husky. "You forget. I'm a nanny and I'm scheduled to work next Friday."

"I know your boss pretty well." Drew gently brushed back a strand of her hair with his hand. "I think I can get you some time off."

Books by Cynthia Rutledge

Love Inspired

Unforgettable Faith #102
Undercover Angel #123
The Marrying Kind #135
Redeeming Claire #151
Judging Sara #157
Wedding Bell Blues #178
A Love To Keep #208

Silhouette Romance

Trish's Not-So-Little Secret #1581
Kiss Me, Kaitlyn #1651

CYNTHIA RUTLEDGE

is a lifelong Nebraska resident. She graduated from the University of Nebraska with a liberal arts degree, then returned several years later to earn a degree in nursing. A registered nurse, Cynthia now works full-time for a large insurance company and writes in the evenings and on weekends. She loves writing romance because a happy ending is guaranteed! An author of seven books for Steeple Hill's Love Inspired series, Cynthia has also written two books for Silhouette Romance.

Cynthia loves to hear from readers and encourages you to visit her Web site at:
http://www.cynthiarutledge.com.

A LOVE
TO KEEP

CYNTHIA RUTLEDGE

Published by Steeple Hill Books™

STEEPLE HILL BOOKS

Steeple
Hill™

ISBN 0-373-87215-1

A LOVE TO KEEP

Copyright © 2003 by Cynthia Rutledge

This edition published by arrangement with Steeple Hill Books.

® and TM are trademarks of Steeple Hill Books, used under license. Trademarks indicated with ® are registered in the United States Patent and Trademark Office, the Canadian Trade Marks Office and in other countries.

Visit us at www.steeplehill.com

Printed in U.S.A.

Two are better than one,
If one falls down, his friend can help him up.
But pity the man who falls and has
no one to help him up!
Also, if two lie down together, they will keep warm.
But how can one keep warm alone?
A cord of three strands is not quickly broken.
—*Ecclesiastes* 4: 9-12

To my critique partner, Louise Foster.
You're the best!

Chapter One

American Teen

Dear Lorelei Love,
My father is being transferred and my parents say we have to move to another state. I don't want to leave my friends. What can I do?
                    Bummed in Birmingham

Dear Bummed,
I'll soon be moving to a new city, too. Moving to a new place can be scary. But it can also be exciting. A chance to start fresh with people who don't know you threw up on the bus in third grade or that you were the only girl who didn't have a date to the freshman

formal. Try to think of this move as an exciting adventure and chances are that's just
what it will be.

LL

"I'm sorry I've kept you waiting."

Lorelei Loveland turned and her breath caught
in her throat. Though she knew it was impolite to
stare, Lori couldn't help herself. Ever since she'd
been a teenager she'd had a weakness for dark-
haired guys with bright blue eyes.

"I was on a conference call and it went longer
than I expected." The man smiled and strode
across the study.

When he stopped in front of her, Lori noticed
there were flecks of gold in the blue depths, and
when he smiled a little dimple flashed in his left
cheek. Her heart skipped a beat.

He extended his hand. "It's a pleasure to finally
put a face with a voice."

Lori took his hand, liking the firmness of his
grip and the way he measured her with a cool assessing look. She met his gaze, her hand lingering
in his. "You're not at all what I expected."

The man before her didn't look anything like the
boring middle-aged executive she'd envisioned.
And he certainly didn't look like anyone's father.
Her hopes rose. Maybe being a nanny for the next
six months wouldn't be so bad after all....

"Excuse me for interrupting."

Lori turned. The petite gray-haired housekeeper who'd shown her to the study stood in the doorway.

Mr. McCashlin lifted a brow. "Yes, Mrs. Graham?"

"Sir, Ms. Tobin is on the phone and insists on speaking with you."

"Tell her I'm in a meeting," he said without a hint of hesitation. "I'll have to call her back."

"Very well." The housekeeper slipped out of the room as silently as she'd entered.

Lori took a sip of iced tea and glanced around the spacious room. Cherry-wood shelves filled with leather-bound books covered the far wall. A painting that looked suspiciously like an Antonio Varas hung above a large executive desk. "You have a beautiful home, Mr. McCashlin."

"Please call me Drew." The dimple flashed again. "Mr. McCashlin is so formal."

"Only if you call me Lori." She offered him her most engaging smile. Flirting with an employer was never a good idea, but she told herself she wasn't really flirting. She was just being friendly.

"I know I shouldn't say this—" Drew paused "—but Clay never told me you were so pretty."

"Then we're even," Lori said. "Because he never told me you were so handsome, either."

She thought he would be used to such compliments but, though Drew laughed easily, a touch of red crept up his neck. Lori found the lack of conceit refreshing.

"So what *did* Clay tell you about me?" she asked.

That cute little dimple reappeared in his cheek. "He said you were a hard worker, loved children and had a wonderful sense of humor."

"I always knew I liked him," she said with a saucy smile.

"But the way he described you," Drew continued, "I didn't think you'd be so young."

"I'm not that young," Lori said, remembering the over-the-hill birthday cake at her last party. "I hit the big three-oh last month."

"Wow." His eyes widened in mock surprise. "You'll be getting those senior discounts in no time."

"Stop it." Lori couldn't help but respond to the twinkle in his eye.

He laughed and took a seat in the chair opposite hers. "I'd hate to hear what you consider forty-three to be."

"Positively ancient," she said promptly, tossing him a smile to show she was only teasing. Because Drew McCashlin was anything but ancient. His dark brown hair didn't have a trace of gray and the only wrinkles she could detect were a few laugh lines around his eyes and mouth. "Seriously, if I didn't know Clay, I'd never believe you had a grown son."

"Sometimes even I can't believe it. Karen and I were just kids ourselves when he was born." Drew shook his head. "We married right out of high school. Clay was born nine months later."

His eyes took on a faraway look and Lori had the feeling she knew just what he was thinking. She'd heard all about the tragic accident that had claimed Karen McCashlin's life.

"I'm sorry about your wife," Lori said in a low tone. "Clay said she died in a car accident a few years ago?"

"It'll be two years next month." Drew's gaze shifted to the window. "She and our youngest daughter were on I-90 during a thunderstorm. A drunk driver swerved into their lane. Karen couldn't avoid a collision. When I got that phone call…"

He rubbed a hand across his face and Lori's heart ached in sympathy. Though she'd never been married, never lost a spouse, she understood what it was like to get such news. She'd been twelve when her father's semi had jackknifed on an icy road.

"At the time you think it's the end of the world," she murmured, almost to herself.

"It was horrible," Drew said quietly. "But I'm

grateful Molly was spared. For a while we thought we might lose her, too.''

"Holly is your youngest daughter, right?"

"Actually, it's Molly." A ghost of a smile crossed his lips.

Lori stifled a groan. First day on the job and she'd already blown the child's name. She smiled brightly. "I understand you have two daughters?"

"That's right." Drew leaned back in his chair. "Nicole is my oldest girl. She's a junior in high school and very independent. She acts like she's sixteen going on thirty."

"Thirty?" Lori grinned. "Then we should get along just fine."

Drew smiled. "I think you'll like both girls."

"I'm sure I will," Lori said. "I can't wait to meet them."

"Before you do, there's something you should know." Drew leaned forward and clasped his hands together. "Molly is a very sweet girl, but ever since the accident..."

A sense of unease traveled up Lori's spine at his hesitation. When her friends had told her she should have gotten more information about the girls before she'd accepted the position, she'd pooh-poohed their concerns. Now she wished she'd asked a few more questions.

"Molly hasn't said a word since the accident," he said at last.

Lori's jaw dropped open. She shut it with a snap. "She doesn't talk?"

"She did before the accident," he said. "Not since."

"But that was two years ago." Lori couldn't hide her surprise.

"I know." Drew drew a heavy, pained sigh.

"Is it that she doesn't *want* to talk?" Lori probed gently. "Or that she *can't?*"

"Physically, there's nothing wrong. The doctors say she'll talk when she's ready." Drew shook his head.

"Losing a parent is devastating for a child," Lori said. "My father died when I was twelve and I can't tell you how much I missed him."

"Then you do understand." Relief sounded in Drew's voice. "I know Clay said you had a background in child psychology, but I never knew you'd experienced the loss of a parent."

"It's not something that usually comes up in casual conversations." Lori lifted one shoulder in a slight shrug.

"If you don't mind my asking, what helped you the most during that time?" he asked. "Was it something someone said? Or did?"

For a second Lori was tempted to toss off some platitude about time healing all wounds. But Drew had been honest with her. She could be no less with him.

"I'd have to say my faith. Though I don't talk a lot about it, it's something that has really helped me get through many difficult times."

"My wife felt that way, too," Drew responded. "But in the end, when she really needed His help, God wasn't there for her."

Lori opened her mouth to argue the point. To tell him that God would never have forsaken his wife in her darkest hour. But she could tell by his closed expression that he wasn't ready to listen.

"Another thing that helped was the fact that my brothers and sisters needed me," she said. "I'm the oldest of six, and after my dad died, I had to take care of the house and my younger siblings."

"Not many twelve-year-olds could handle such responsibility," Drew pointed out.

"I didn't have much choice," Lori said matter-of-factly. "My mother had to work. She needed the help."

"At least it didn't turn you off children."

"What do you mean?"

"I mean you must like children to want to be a nanny."

This time it was Lori's turn to hesitate. Telling Drew that her decision to take care of his children was based purely on financial considerations didn't seem wise. And, anyway, it wouldn't be entirely true.

"I find children, especially adolescents, fascinating.'' It was that fascination that had led her to her current position as a writer for *American Teen* magazine. ''Did I ever tell you about the column I—''

The door to the study swung unexpectedly open and Drew's gaze shifted. His smile widened. ''Molly, sweetheart. Come in and meet Miss Loveland. She's going to be your new nanny.''

Lori turned in her seat.

A girl with long blond hair and her father's blue eyes stood in the doorway. Dressed in a hot pink sundress, she looked to Lori's discerning eye to be no more than seven. But unlike Lori's brothers and sisters, who'd been noisy, lively children at that age, Molly stood silent, her watchful gaze shifting between her father and Lori.

''Hello, Molly.'' This time Lori made sure she got the name right. ''Are you having a nice summer?''

Molly smiled and ducked her head shyly. She crossed the room to her father and he pulled her onto his lap. The little girl relaxed in his arms, but her gaze remained fixed on Lori. The look in her eyes was curious and intense, but not unfriendly.

Two down. One to go.

If Nicole were half as nice as her father and sister, the next six months would be a breeze.

And though Lori had never been one to wish her

life away, the rest of the year couldn't go by quickly enough. Only then would her real life begin.

Drew waited until Lori had left the room to unpack, and Molly had headed outside to play, before shutting the door and picking up the phone. He quickly dialed the familiar number.

"Clay McCashlin."

"Clay, it's your dad." Drew leaned back in the leather desk chair. "I thought you might want to know Lori arrived safely. She's upstairs unpacking now."

"Isn't she great?" His son's voice warmed.

"She seems very nice," Drew said grudgingly, knowing it was an understatement, but unwilling to admit just how much she'd impressed him. "But she isn't quite what I expected."

"What do you mean?"

"I expected an older woman. Someone—" Drew searched for the right word "—matronly."

"Matronly?" A trace of amusement laced Clay's words. "I never said Lori was matronly."

"No. But you didn't tell me she was just a kid, either." Drew stood, suddenly unable to sit any longer. "She's young enough to be my daughter."

"She is not." Clay laughed. "And even if she were, what does it matter?"

"Age brings a certain amount of experience," Drew said. "You know Alice was a grandmother."

"So? Molly hated the old hag," Clay said. "The woman wouldn't play with her or take her to the park or anything."

"That's beside the point." Drew moved to the window and brushed the curtain aside with one hand.

"Then what is the point?"

"If she just weren't so pretty." Drew let the drapery fall shut and heaved an audible sigh. He didn't need this kind of complication in his life.

"Ahh," Clay said. "Now I understand. You're worried about Susan's reaction."

"That's not it at all," Drew said. He hadn't even considered what his current girlfriend would think about Lori. Drew rarely thought of Susan in between social engagements, and today had been no exception.

No, it wasn't Susan's feelings that were the problem. It was his own.

Lori spent the afternoon unpacking and getting her "room" in order. After seeing the house, she'd expected her accommodations to be nice, but she'd never imagined anything quite this grand.

The bedroom was really more like a suite, with its own adjoining bath and sitting room. Though Lori was by no means an expert at estimating square foot-

age, her new living quarters had to be at least as big
as the apartment she'd had back home.

But though the space might have been similar,
there was no comparison between the two. Her
apartment in Iowa had been filled with furniture
bought at estate auctions and decorated with ideas
gleaned from supermarket magazines. Everyone
said she had a flare for bringing out the best in a
room, but Lori was the first to admit she was no
professional.

Not like the person who'd decorated this room.

Her gaze shifted from the stylish window treat-
ments that complemented the bedspread to the
hand-painted flowers that enhanced the pale yellow
walls. This was not the work of an amateur. A
professional had clearly created the magic in this
room.

Though it wasn't entirely unexpected that a man
of Drew McCashlin's stature would own such a
house or avail himself of an interior designer's services, it was another piece of the puzzle that didn't
quite fit with what his son had told her.

Clay had said his father was a good guy but
somewhat of a tightwad. Said he drove an old
Chevy pickup and rarely ate out. Said he got ten-
dollar haircuts and would never consider paying
money to get his shoes shined.

Based on that information, Lori had came to
Chicago with certain expectations. Expectations

that had been blown out of the water the minute she'd seen the house and met the man.

Though the Tudor-inspired manor house wasn't elaborate for a man of Drew's wealth, its marble fireplaces, exposed-beam ceilings and leaded-glass windows placed it in a different class from the spartan residence she'd envisioned.

And if his house was nothing like she'd expected, Drew wasn't what she'd expected, either. It had been a long time since she'd met a man who'd piqued her interest so thoroughly.

It was just too bad he had children. If he didn't, despite their age difference, she might have been interested. He was certainly attractive and she liked his personality, the way he'd gently teased her, his concern over his daughter. But the bottom line was he had two children still living at home. And it would be aeons before Molly was grown.

The last thing Lori wanted to do was to spend another ten years of her life raising someone else's children. She'd been down that road once and she wasn't interested in going down it again.

She'd been a good daughter and a good sister. She'd put the good of others before her own. But now it was her turn. And if that made her selfish, so be it.

Chapter Two

American Teen

Dear Lorelei Love,
I was at a party last weekend and suddenly across the room—there he was! He came over and said hi but it was all I could do to keep breathing. Do you believe in love at first sight? What should I say to him when I see him in the halls at school?

> Lovestruck in Louisiana

Dear Lovestruck,
It's an awesome experience when that lightning bolt hits. You see him and the attraction is instantly there. When you brush up against him or you touch his hand, the electrical

surge could light a city block. Is it love? Not yet. But it certainly is a good start. What should you do now? Start by saying hello. If he's on a sports team, say something about the last game. Or ask him for his algebra notes. Take time to get to know him. Only then will you know if he's the guy for you.

LL

Lori glanced around the room and smiled in satisfaction. Her dresses hung freshly pressed in the spacious walk-in closet. The dresser drawers were filled with neatly folded clothes. And her laptop was out and ready.

Although her deadline for her next *American Teen* column wasn't due for another two weeks, Lori was anxious to get started. She still couldn't believe they were paying her to give advice.

She'd done articles for the teen magazine on a freelance basis for several years and knew they'd liked her work. But to actually snag a regular monthly slot, giving advice to young girls, had been beyond her wildest dreams.

When they'd offered her the position, Lori had done some quick calculations and discovered if she was careful, she'd be able to support herself on the writing alone. And best of all, it gave her the excuse to move to Chicago.

But moving wasn't cheap, so when Clay had

told her his dad was looking for a nanny and would pay relocation to the Windy City, her ears had perked up. When she'd called Mr. McCashlin and learned he was only asking for a six-month commitment, her heart had picked up speed. And when he named the salary and said she'd have free room and board, she'd said yes immediately. She could easily take care of two children and still have time to write.

Eager to get started, Lori took a seat at the desk by the window and booted up the computer. Before long her fingers were flying across the keyboard.

"Miss Loveland?"

Lori stopped midsentence. Even though the thick hardwood muffled the words, she immediately recognized the voice. She rose, crossed the room and opened the door. "Yes?"

Mrs. Graham stood in the hall. Though she was barely five feet tall, the housekeeper reminded Lori of a drill sergeant with her ramrod-straight posture and take-no-prisoners attitude.

"The family will be dining early this evening. Mr. McCashlin requests your presence in the dining room at six." Mrs. Graham's expression was inscrutable.

"Join the family?" Lori didn't even try to hide her surprise. "I didn't think nannies usually ate with the family."

Before leaving Shelby, Iowa, Lori had talked with several women who'd been nannies. Though she knew each household did things a little differently, she'd expected to eat with the other staff in the kitchen.

The housekeeper ignored Lori's comment. Her gaze flicked over the shorts and T-shirt Lori had changed into while unpacking. "I think I should tell you that although the family doesn't dress for dinner per se, I'd suggest—"

"I'll change."

"Good."

The woman turned to go but Lori reached out and stopped her. "Mrs. Graham."

The housekeeper raised one finely arched brow. "Yes, Miss Loveland?"

"Thanks for giving me the heads-up about proper dinner attire." Though Lori knew she never would have showed up dressed so casually, she still appreciated the housekeeper's concern.

"It's all part of my job, Miss Loveland."

"Still, I appreciate it." Lori wondered if the woman was always this formal. She hoped not. Otherwise it would be a long six months. "And please, call me Lori."

"If you insist." Mrs. Graham nodded.

"And what shall I call you?" Lori asked as the woman once again turned to leave.

"You may call me—" the housekeeper paused and a hint of a smile touched her lips "—Mrs. Graham."

Drew jerked off the Valentino tie his son had given him for his birthday and tossed it on the bed. The last thing he wanted was to look like he'd dressed to impress the new nanny. Even the thought was ridiculous.

Unbuttoning his shirt, he pulled it off and exchanged it for the navy polo he'd discarded only moments earlier. Before he could change his mind, Drew slipped on a pair of chinos and headed down the stairs.

He'd just seated Molly at the table when Lori appeared in the doorway. For a moment, all he could do was stare. Though tasteful and demure, the sleeveless black dress showed off an amazing expanse of honey-colored skin. Regretfully, he thought of the shirt and tie lying on his bed. "You look lovely this evening."

Her hand hesitantly rose to her neck, fingering a strand of pearls. Her gaze shifted from his polo shirt to his chinos. "Mrs. Graham said to dress for dinner. I think I might have overdone it...."

"Not at all. What you have on is just perfect," he said honestly.

For a long moment she stared, her gaze searching his. Then she smiled and it was as if the sun had broken through the clouds.

Feeling strangely lighthearted, Drew waited for her to be seated then pushed in her chair.

Mrs. Graham entered the room and cast him a questioning look.

Drew took his seat and nodded. With a business meeting at seven-thirty, they had to stay on schedule if they wanted a leisurely meal.

The housekeeper hesitated. Her gaze shifted to the empty chair. ''Sir, Miss Nicole isn't here yet.''

''Nicole knows we're eating at six. Just because she's late is no reason—''

''Who's late?'' Like a breath of fresh air, his oldest daughter breezed into the room, her cheeks rosy from the summer sun. With her dark hair and almond-shaped hazel eyes, Nicole was the spitting image of his late wife.

''You are,'' he said, casting a glance at the clock on the mantel.

''Big deal.'' Nicole plopped into the chair and dropped the napkin onto her lap. ''I'm here now, aren't I?''

Drew bit his tongue and reminded himself Nicole was only being a typical teen by asserting her independence.

''Who's she?'' Nicole tilted her head and gazed speculatively at Lori.

Drew's gaze shifted from Nicole to Lori. He gave Lori a reassuring smile. ''This is Lori Loveland, the new nanny. Lori, this is my daughter Nicole.''

Lori smiled pleasantly. ''It's nice to meet you.''

But Nicole didn't return the smile. Instead her brow furrowed and her gaze riveted to her father. ''I thought we agreed we didn't need another nanny.''

''Honey, you and I both know that wouldn't have worked.'' Drew kept his voice calm and level. Nicole and he had argued long and hard about his decision to hire another nanny. She'd begged him not to fill the position, arguing that if she shared Molly's care with him, they could make it work.

''I told you I didn't mind.'' Nicole leaned forward, resting her arms on the table, her expression earnest. ''I'll have a lot of free time this summer—''

''Honey, we'll talk about this later.'' Drew cast a pointed glance in Lori's direction.

''But I want to talk about it now.'' Nicole's jaw set in that stubborn tilt he'd grown to know so well. ''And why is she eating with us anyway? You've always told us dinner is family time. She's not a member of this family.''

''Maybe it *would* be best if I ate in the kitchen.'' Lori pushed back her chair.

Drew's temper inched up a notch. He gestured

for Lori to remain seated and his gaze pinned Nicole. "You owe Miss Loveland an apology."

"What should I apologize for?" Nicole met his gaze without flinching. "Telling the truth?"

Drew took a deep breath and counted to ten. He'd learned in the past two years that raising his voice to Nicole only made matters worse. But he couldn't let such rude behavior go unchecked.

The door from the kitchen opened and Mrs. Graham entered the room balancing a silver tray. With minimal movement and utmost efficiency, the older woman placed plates of salad before them, ignoring the fact that Drew and Nicole were glaring at each other across the table.

"You *will* apologize," Drew said.

"I won't." Nicole's chin inched higher. "And you can't make me."

"Mrs. Graham." Though he spoke to the housekeeper, Drew kept his gaze focused on Nicole. "My daughter will be dining in her room this evening."

"I have more right than she does to sit at this table." Though her words were bold, Nicole's bottom lip trembled and Drew knew she was more upset than she was letting on. He just couldn't understand why.

"Nonetheless," he said, firmly, "tonight you'll be eating in your room."

"Fine." Nicole jumped to her feet and threw her

napkin on the table, scattering salad across the white linen surface. Her palm slapped the door open on her way out of the room.

Drew took a deep breath and slowly released it, sorely tempted to go after her. But he hesitated. Although he might win the battle, he had the unsettling feeling he could lose the war.

It was times like these that made him wonder if he was capable of raising two girls alone. He cast Lori an apologetic smile. "Sorry."

"Is she always like that?" Lori lifted a brow.

"Not always." Drew heaved a sigh. "Sometimes she's worse."

Nicole wiped the tears from her eyes with the back of her hand and resisted the urge to slam down the phone. What good were friends if they weren't around when you needed them?

She'd forgotten Erin had left this morning to spend the summer with her father in Massachusetts. Nicole had the phone number, but this was her friend's first night there and she doubted Erin would see this issue as a crisis.

She could hear her friend now, asking her what the big deal was? So she had another nanny. She'd had one before.

Actually, they'd had three since her mother died. And Nicole hadn't been sad to see any of them go. She didn't like strangers hanging around.

When she'd seen the new nanny at the dinner table, a shiver of fear had crept up her spine. None of the others had eaten dinner with the family. Having this one at the table was a bad sign. A really bad sign.

Though her father kept saying that she and Molly were his priority now, Nicole worried he was slipping back into his old habits. Tonight he'd said he was too busy to take care of Molly. What would be next?

Was he bringing this new woman in to eat dinner with them so when he started working late again, she and Molly wouldn't have to eat alone?

"Nicole." Her dad's voice came from the hall outside her bedroom door. "May I come in?"

Nicole could hear a hint of apology in his tone and her spirits rose. Maybe he'd changed his mind. Maybe he'd realized he'd made a mistake. Maybe he was coming to tell her that Lucy, or whatever the new nanny's name was, would be gone before morning.

"Just a minute." Nicole jumped to her feet, unlocked the door and returned to sit cross-legged on the bed. "It's open."

He pushed the door open and stood there, his brow creased with worry and an all-too-familiar sadness in his gaze.

Despite her determination not to give an inch,

Nicole wanted nothing more than to do whatever it took to put the old light back in his eyes.

"We need to talk about what happened at the table," he said quietly.

Just as quickly as Nicole's hopes had risen, they crashed. This wasn't going to be a "goodbye nanny" talk at all. It was the more familiar "I'm so disappointed in your behavior" talk.

He gestured to a chair next to the bed. "Mind if I sit down?"

Nicole lifted one shoulder in a half shrug. "It's your house."

Lifting the stuffed raccoon from the chair, Drew took a seat, flashing Nicole a conciliatory smile.

It took all her willpower not to return the smile.

His smile faded. He shifted his gaze to the raccoon in his lap. "Remember when your mother bought this for you? You must have been about Molly's age."

"I was eight," Nicole said, ignoring the sudden tightness gripping her chest. "I was sad because Clay was going off to college and Mom bought it to cheer me up."

"You and your mother were very close," he said softly. "I know you still miss her."

Nicole nodded and lowered her gaze.

"We all miss her." He stopped and cleared his throat. "I want you to know I understand why you acted the way you did."

"You do?" Nicole's eyes widened.

"I thought about it all through dinner until it finally hit me. Lori was sitting in your mother's place." His gaze softened. "I realize now how that must have looked. I'm so sorry."

For a second, Nicole was too stunned to speak. Where her father had gotten such a crazy notion was beyond her. But he obviously felt bad and she decided to use that to her advantage.

"It *was* hard," Nicole said, pleased her voice came out low and husky. "Seeing her sitting there like she was part of the family."

"Oh, honey." Her father leaned forward and took her hand. "Today is Lori's first day as a nanny here. I just wanted her to feel comfortable, as well as get to know you girls a bit. I'm not interested in her."

"I should hope not." Shocked, Nicole forgot the need to measure her words. "She's way too young for you."

For a moment she thought her dad was going to protest. But that would have been crazy. Though she'd barely spared the woman at the table a second glance, Nicole knew the nanny couldn't be much older than her brother. Just the thought that her father might be interested in such a woman was laughable.

"I'm sorry I got so upset...." Nicole let her words trail off.

"I'm sorry, too." He paused. "How about we go out for ice cream or something?"

"She's not coming with us, is she?"

Her father shook his head. "No, it will be just the three of us."

Just the three of us. It took all the restraint Nicole had to keep a satisfied smile from her lips. "What about your meeting?"

"I canceled it," he said. "I'd rather spend the evening with my two favorite girls."

"A burger does sound good."

"I'm thinking hot fudge sundae."

They exchanged a smile. Before he left the room to make a phone call, Nicole gave him a quick hug, just to show there were no hard feelings.

He closed the door behind him and Nicole plopped back on the bed, heaving a sigh of relief.

The nanny might not be out the door yet, but she *would* be.

Soon.

Very soon.

Chapter Three

American Teen

Dear Lorelei Love,
I'm fifteen and my brother is three. Lately my parents have started expecting me to watch him when they go out on the week-ends. Don't they realize I have a life to live, too? I don't mind helping out, but every week? Enough is enough! What should I do?
Fuming in Florida

Dear Fuming,
I understand where you're coming from. Though I'm a firm believer that family members should help each other out, it sounds like your parents are taking advantage of you. I

suggest you find a time and talk with them about your concerns. But I'd do it at a time other than when they're asking you to baby-sit. :) You could tell them you wouldn't mind baby-sitting one weekend a month, or even more if you're not busy, but you're only young once. Just present your case in a calm rational manner and chances are they'll get the picture. Good luck!

LL

Lori couldn't keep from smiling as she flipped through her closet searching for the perfect dress. She could hardly believe it. Only two weeks in Chicago and she already had a date! The strange thing was, it was her nanny job that had brought her and Tom Bowers together.

Tom was the stepbrother of one of Molly's girl-friends. Lori had met him when she'd taken Molly over to play with Jasmyn. But instead of dropping off Molly and coming back later, she'd ended up staying and talking to Tom. When he'd asked for her phone number, she'd thought he was just being polite. But to her surprise, he'd called the next day.

A tiny part of her still felt bad she'd had to turn Drew down when he'd asked if she could watch Molly tonight. But the other part was glad she'd had a reason to say no. After all, it *was* Saturday night and, despite what her birthday balloons had said last month, she wasn't "over the hill" yet. She had a lot of living to do before she settled down.

Tom had told her to dress up. After an obligatory appearance at his parents' party, he'd promised to take her somewhere "extra nice." Lori had been tempted to ask him where a graduate student who didn't work got the money for somewhere "extra nice," but she decided she already knew the answer. The Lake Forest mansion where Jasmyn and his parents lived had told her all she needed to know.

Her fingers stopped on the black scoop-neck Yves Saint Laurent dress. Lori pulled it from the closet and critically assessed it. Though she'd picked it up at a designer consignment store in Des Moines, it looked brand-new.

Lori laid the dress carefully on the bed and turned to her jewelry box. She rummaged through the chest until she found the perfect accessory: a moonstone necklace she'd inherited from her grandmother.

Ten minutes later, she gazed in the mirror and smiled in satisfaction. The hot rollers had done their job, imparting a little, but not too much, curl. And the dress fit beautifully.

Confident that she looked her best, Lori skillfully applied a touch of lipstick and headed out the door.

Tom had balked when she'd insisted on meeting him at his parents' house, but she knew it had been the right decision. Though she firmly believed men should pick up their dates, having Tom pick her up at Drew's home would have been awkward.

When Drew had asked her to watch Molly because of some last-minute "business engagement," she'd only told him she'd had a previous commitment. Though he'd seemed surprised at her refusal, he hadn't tried to change her mind. But if Tom *had* shown up at the door, Drew would have known that her "previous commitment" was nothing more than a date.

Drew made sure Susan was safely inside the Passat before he shut the door. He rounded the front of the car and slipped behind the wheel. Though the small vehicle was very nice, he missed the roominess of his pickup. If it were up to him, they'd be in that spacious club cab now. With full leather interior and a dynamite sound system, the 1985 Chevy looked as if it could have come off a showroom floor.

But Susan hated the truck with a passion, so he'd made the sacrifice and borrowed Nicole's Volkswagen for the evening.

For the first few blocks, Susan did all the talking. She chattered on about some new philanthropic campaign she was chairing and Drew contented himself with an occasional nod or smile.

The party they were attending was black-tie, and though Drew hated "dressing up" himself, he'd always liked women in evening dresses. Tonight was no exception.

Susan looked positively elegant. Her gown was an interesting shade of copper that brought out the hint of red in her hair and made her brown eyes look almost gold. The fabric was some shiny material that shimmered in the dim light of the car. But the best part of the dress was the way it was cut. For a woman who wore only the most conservative of business suits ninety-five percent of the time, the dress showed a surprising amount of cleavage.

"I like your dress," he said when she paused to take a breath.

"It's a Loris Azzaro," she said, her face lighting with pleasure at his compliment. "And the necklace is a Neil Lane."

Drew recognized the designer names. Karen had been into such things. Though he personally thought people got too caught up in that kind of stuff, he was the only one among his friends and family who felt that way.

His gaze returned to the dress. "Worth every penny."

"I'm so glad you decided to come." Susan's

smile widened. "Though I still don't understand what made you change your mind."

Drew shrugged. "I saw Rod at a meeting downtown and he mentioned how much he and Gayle were looking forward to having me over. I thought I'd better show up."

"It's going to be a fabulous party," Susan said. "I hope you won't have to leave early."

Drew slanted a sideways glance. "Why would I have to leave early?"

"You know—" Susan waved one hand in the air "—the children."

"I've got that base covered," Drew said. "Tonight we can stay as late as we want."

"I knew I'd like that new nanny of yours," Susan said with a pleased smile. "By the way, how is she doing?"

"She's working out." Drew paused. "But tonight she had plans, so Nicole is baby-sitting."

"Really?" Susan raised a brow. "I bet the princess was thrilled about that."

"She didn't mind." He tried to keep his irritation from showing. For not the first time, Drew wished Susan had a better understanding of teenagers. Because, regardless of how it sounded at times, Nicole was a normal sixteen-year-old and a good kid. "She's always offering to help with Molly."

"If you say so," Susan said. "But tell me again why the nanny couldn't watch the young one?"

"She was busy," he said. "Tonight is her night off, so I didn't feel right asking her to change her plans."

"You gave her a Saturday night off?" Susan shook her head. "You're too generous, Drew. You need to schedule her hours so it works best for you."

Drew concentrated on his driving and remained silent. He'd never been one to appreciate unsolicited advice.

"Okay, don't change her hours." Susan heaved a resigned sigh. "Thankfully, I have another option for you. My friend Patrice uses a baby-sitting service and she loves it. I'll be glad to get you the name."

"Don't bother," Drew said. "Molly doesn't like strangers."

"She'd get to know them. The one Patrice uses only hires workers with education degrees," Susan said. "They're very reputable."

"I'm sure they are," Drew said in a calm tone that belied his rising irritation. "But I don't like the idea of someone I don't know in my home taking care of my child."

"If you feel that way, I'm surprised you hired that new nanny. If I remember correctly, you offered her the job without ever laying eyes on her."

"Clay knew her," Drew said. "My son's recommendation is good enough for me."

"Just give the baby-sitting service a try." Susan trailed a perfectly manicured nail up his sleeve. "I know you'll like it."

"I'm not interested." He spoke slowly and distinctly so there would be no misunderstanding.

Susan's eyes widened at his firm tone and she pulled her hand away. For a moment he thought she was going to foolishly press the point, but instead she smiled. "The party should be fun, don't you think?"

"I'd say it's a virtual certainty considering who's hosting the party." Drew forced an equally pleasant tone. There was no reason they couldn't have a nice evening. After all, they were both reasonable adults. "You know their son Tom is just a few years older than Clay. In fact, they used to play together when they were young."

"I haven't seen Tom in ages. The last I heard he'd given up his place in New York, moved back to Chicago and was back in graduate school at Northwestern."

"I wonder if he'll be here tonight." Drew turned the car into the circular lane leading up to the large Lake Forest estate. "I hope so. It'd be good to see the boy again."

Looking incredibly handsome in his tux, Thomas Bowers confiscated a couple of flutes of champagne from a passing waiter and handed one to Lori.

She smiled her thanks and took a sip. Her gaze shifted around the room. It slid past the quartet of musicians playing softly in one corner and settled on the room's focal point, a magnificent ice sculpture at least five feet tall.

Lori stared at the intricately carved block of ice and took another sip of the champagne. This was the kind of party she'd dreamed of attending all those years when she'd been reading bedtime stories to her sisters and wiping her brothers' noses. "This is a lovely party."

"It's okay." Tom shrugged and downed his champagne in one gulp. "If you like hanging out with a bunch of senior citizens."

Lori gaze shifted around the crowded room filled with handsome men in tuxedos and beautiful women in evening gowns. Though there were a handful of guests in their fifties and a few in their sixties, most of the crowd looked to Lori's discerning gaze to be somewhere in their thirties and forties. "They don't look that old to me."

"Just wait." Tom leaned closer, his breath tickling her ear. "By the end of the evening, they'll be exchanging stories about their operations and comparing aches and pains."

Lori took another sip of champagne and peered

at him over the top of the glass. "Does that mean you don't want to hear about the appendectomy I had when I was ten?"

Tom chuckled and his arm slipped possessively around her waist. "Only if you promise to show me your sca—"

"Thomas. I'm so glad you could make it."

Tom stiffened, but when he turned to the blond-haired woman he had a smile on his face. "Hello, Mother."

His mother gave him a quick hug. Her low-cut black dress was stylish and chic and the diamond on her left hand had to be at least three carats.

"And who is this young lady?" The woman turned to Lori and offered her a welcoming smile. "I don't believe we've met."

"Mother, this is Lori Loveland," Tom said. "Lori, this is my mother, Mrs. Bowers."

"Please, call me Gayle."

The two exchanged pleasantries for a few minutes before Gayle excused herself to "mingle."

"Your mother is lovely."

"She's a very nice woman," Tom agreed. "Though she drives me crazy at times. Just wait. Tonight, when we get ready to leave, she'll have to make sure and tell me to drive carefully and buckle my seat belt."

Lori flushed, remembering the admonitions

she'd given her siblings. She started to tell Tom that when he'd be a parent he'd understand, but stopped herself just in time.

Even though she'd helped raise five children, she wasn't a parent. And even though she probably had more in common with most of the people in this room than the young man at her side, she reminded herself she was single. And young. And here to have fun.

Lori slipped her arm through Tom's and took a leisurely sip of champagne. She glanced around the room admiring all the dresses. A shimmery copper-colored one in the entryway caught her eye.

She froze.

It couldn't be.

She blinked and looked again.

Drew stood laughing with Tom's parents, the woman with the beautiful dress at his side.

Lori's pulse skittered alarmingly.

Before she could consider her options, Drew turned. Though there must have been a hundred people in the room, his gaze met hers.

Ignoring the urge to run, Lori lifted her chin, took another sip of champagne and smiled.

Chapter Four

American Teen

Dear Lorelei Love,
My father is always preaching about the evils
of drinking and driving. But I found out he
was arrested for DUI four years ago. I can't
believe he's done the very thing he's warned
me not to do.

Disappointed in Delaware

Dear Disappointed,
Sooner or later everyone in our life will disappoint us. No one is perfect. We all make
mistakes. But if we're smart, we learn from
them. It sounds like that's what your father

has done. Give him a break on this, and hopefully the next time you find yourself in a jam, he'll return the favor.

LL

Drew's gaze narrowed. For a moment he would have sworn he'd seen Lori across the crowded room. But he quickly realized it couldn't be her. A nanny would never run in the same social circle as Rod and Gayle.

Still…

His gaze drifted back. The woman's back was to him now. She was about the right height as Lori with the same silvery blond hair. What was really strange was that the young man at her side looked familiar, too.

"Tom's changed a lot these last few years," Gayle said, apparently noticing the direction of Drew's gaze. "He's not my little boy anymore."

"That's Tom?" Drew widened his gaze, unable to hide his surprise. Somehow he'd expected Tom to still be the boy he remembered. "He looks so old. It seems like only yesterday that he and Clay were fighting over what Nintendo game to play."

Gayle laughed. "Thankfully, they grew up."

Susan leaned around him, her brow furrowed in a slight frown. "Who's that with him? She doesn't look familiar."

"Her name is Lori Loveland," Gayle said.

"Tom's quite taken with her. They met about a month ago."

Drew thought about saying it couldn't have been a month ago because Lori had only been in Chicago two weeks, but he held his tongue. As far as he was concerned, a man always learned more by listening than by hearing himself talk.

"She's very pretty," Susan said grudgingly. "If you like blondes, that is."

"They've always been my favorite." Rod cast a loving glance at his wife. "Doesn't Gayle's hair remind you of sun-ripened wheat?"

"Honey—" Gayle brushed a piece of lint off her husband's sleeve "—your farm roots are showing."

Rod smiled good-naturedly. "Some men like Drew prefer brunettes. I just happen to have a thing for blondes."

Drew smiled, neither agreeing nor disagreeing. Though it was true he'd married a brunette, that didn't mean he couldn't appreciate a good-looking blonde.

He turned to Susan. "Care to dance?"

Susan smiled. "I'd love to."

It was just a coincidence, Drew decided, that they ended up dancing close to where Tom and Lori stood talking to Hugh Claron, one of Drew's business associates.

"Drew McCashlin. Come over here and say hello." The older man's voice boomed.

Susan stiffened in Drew's arms. Appearance was important to his date and Drew could tell Hugh's loud mouth didn't sit well with her. But despite his "good ole boy" demeanor, Hugh Claron was an astute businessman. And a friend.

Drew smiled, acknowledging the silver-haired gentleman. He whirled Susan off the dance floor and joined the threesome.

"No one told me you were coming to this little shindig." Hugh clasped Drew's hand in a firm grip.

"I wasn't sure I was going to be able to attend until the last minute." Drew widened his smile to include Tom and Lori. "But I'm glad it worked out."

Tom extended his hand. "It's nice to see you again, Mr. McCashlin."

When Tom introduced Lori, Drew wasn't sure how he should respond. If only he knew if Lori had told Tom she worked for him. Thankfully, Susan jumped into the momentary silence.

"What do you do, Miss Loveland?" Susan's polite smile didn't quite reach her eyes. "Do you attend Northwestern with Tom?"

"No, I'm finished with higher education. At least for the moment." Lori held a glass of wine loosely in one hand and Drew couldn't help but admire her long red nails. "I write a monthly advice column for *American Teen* magazine and I'm also a nanny. Between the two I don't know when I'd have time for school."

"You're a nanny?" Susan's eyes widened. "Really?"

Lori smiled. "That's right."

"Who do you work for?" Hugh asked. "Anyone we know?"

Lori cast a sideways glance at Drew. "Actually, I'm a nanny for Molly and Nicole, Mr. McCashlin's children."

Susan's face paled. Her gaze swiveled to Drew. "This is your new nanny?"

Hugh threw back his head and laughed. "Drew, you sly dog. What other secrets have you been keeping from us?"

"I'm not sure what you're talking about, Hugh." Drew smiled easily, forcing a casual tone. "I haven't been keeping secrets. Ms. Loveland is a good friend of Clay's and the children adore her."

The last part wasn't entirely true, but Drew still had hopes Nicole would come around.

"Now I remember." Susan's gaze narrowed. "You're Clay's friend. From that little town."

"Shelby, Iowa," Lori said. "Clay's wife and I are best friends."

"How nice," Susan said. A calculating look

filled her gaze. "If you and Tom keep dating, the four of you could double."

"Exactly my thoughts," Tom said, looping his arm proprietarily about Lori's shoulders.

Drew's stomach knotted at the familiarity. "The only problem with that picture is that Clay and Kaitlyn aren't in Chicago. They're back in Shelby."

"I would have thought he'd be too busy getting that new business started to take time off now," Tom said.

"Kaitlyn's father had hip surgery," Lori explained. "He's recovering but he still needs help."

"That doesn't explain what Clay's doing there," Susan said.

"Obviously the boy's in love and wants to be with his wife." Hugh laughed. "I think we all remember what that's like."

Drew's heart twisted. He remembered all too well that wonderful feeling.

"Love is all fine and good," Susan said with a smile. "But we all have responsibilities, and being in love doesn't negate our obligations."

"I don't think you have to worry about those two shirking their responsibilities, Susan." Drew kept his tone light. "They have their priorities straight. And right now, Kaitlyn's father is the priority."

"I'm surprised to hear you place family before

business, Drew," Hugh said. "If I remember correctly, for you it's always been the other way around. Weren't you the guy who missed your own daughter's birth because of a merger agreement?"

"Mr. Kuwamoto was leaving for Japan the next day," Drew said, automatically giving them the same explanation he'd given Karen all those years ago. "If I didn't get the papers signed that day, the merger would have fallen apart. There was a lot of money and a lot of jobs riding on that deal."

At the time his rationale had made perfect sense. But Drew regretted missing Molly's entry into the world. Still, that mistake was in the past and there was nothing he could do now to change it.

"Wasn't that the deal that propelled you into the microprocessor market?" Tom's eyes were bright with interest.

Grateful for the change of subject, Drew related some history behind that whole venture. But the look in Lori's eyes told him she believed what he already knew: no reason was good enough to excuse his behavior.

"She's very pretty." Susan gazed at Drew across the darkened car interior.

"Who?" Drew asked with a nonchalant innocence, pretending he hadn't noticed the glint of jealousy in Susan's eye every time she looked at Lori.

"Your new nanny," Susan said. "Lo-ri Love-land."

Susan said the name in a singsong manner, wrinkling her nose at the end. "Sounds like a stripper."

"Susan." Drew spoke more sharply than he'd intended. He took a deep breath and forced a reasonable tone. "Lori is a nice woman. I won't have you saying anything bad about her."

Susan's gaze lingered on his face. "You like her, don't you? If you didn't, you wouldn't care what I said."

"You forget," Drew said, his grip tightening on the steering wheel, "the woman you're disparaging takes care of my children. She's also a friend of my son's. I'd say there was something wrong if I *didn't* defend her."

Susan looked at him for a long moment. "Perhaps you're right."

"I'm always right," Drew said with a slight smile.

"I don't know about that." Susan chuckled. "But after hearing that story about the Kuwamoto deal, I do know you're one shrewd businessman."

Drew was surprised to hear admiration in her voice. He would have thought that with her being a woman she'd have condemned the very behavior she seemed to admire.

But then he'd never been able to figure Susan out. And sometimes he had to wonder why he even tried.

Lori pulled the keys from her purse and unlocked her car before turning back to Tom. In the moonlight's glow, he looked like a young Greek god. She smiled and gazed at him through lowered lashes.

"I had a great time tonight." Tom's finger trailed up her arm.

"I did, too," she said in a low, husky voice.

It had been a storybook evening. After leaving the party, Tom had treated her to a candlelit dinner at an elegant restaurant just off Michigan Avenue. They'd gotten along famously. With a violin playing softly in the background, Tom had kept her laughing with stories of his college years.

While she'd been working and going to night classes, Tom had been living in a fraternity and having fun. But Lori didn't begrudge him the happy memories. She only wished she could have enjoyed that same lifestyle.

But focusing on the past took away from the present. And right now Lori was having too much fun to even waste one precious moment looking back.

Tonight had turned out just as she'd hoped... with one exception. Who'd have thought she'd have run into Drew McCashlin?

Her lips curved up in a smile and Lori couldn't help but chuckle. Drew had been as surprised to see her as she was to see him.

"What's so funny?" Tom moved closer, forcing her body back against the car. The spicy scent of his cologne filled her nostrils and her pulse quickened.

Lori placed her hands flat against his chest. "It's getting late. I should be going."

Tom lowered his head and brushed her lips with his. "You could stay...."

The thought of reminding Tom they'd just met briefly crossed her mind. But she'd been a part of the dating scene long enough to know that most men didn't see the logic in that argument.

She shook her head. "Not tonight."

His gaze searched hers. "Are you sure?"

"Positive," Lori said, softening her refusal with a smile.

For a second she thought Tom was going to argue, but he must have realized it'd be a losing battle. He smiled good-naturedly and gave a swift kiss. "Another time."

During the drive home, Lori realized he hadn't asked her for another date. But he would. She'd seen the look in his eye. He was definitely interested. Once he figured he'd kept her waiting long enough, he'd call.

And when he did call, she'd act surprised. She'd

pretend she'd been so busy she hadn't even missed him. It was silly, but all part of the game she needed to play if she wanted to keep Tom's interest.

"Sorry I'm late." Lori slid into her seat at the dining room table and dropped the linen napkin onto her lap.

She'd seen the girls on her way down the stairs. They'd already finished their breakfast and were headed upstairs to finish getting ready for church.

"I'm surprised you made it up this early." Drew lifted his gaze from his pancakes, his gaze sharp and assessing. "It had to be close to three when you got in."

Lori noted the censure in his tone and thought about telling him she hadn't had a curfew since she'd been sixteen. But he seemed a bit cranky, so she just smiled sweetly and slathered an English muffin with butter. "It was a nice party. Don't you think?"

He took a sip of coffee. "I was surprised to see you there."

Lori reached for the jelly.

"I didn't know you and Tom had been dating."

Though it wasn't a direct question, Lori could tell he expected a response. Lori set the muffin on her plate and lifted her gaze to meet his. "I guess that makes us even. Because I didn't know you were dating Sheryl."

"Sheryl?" Drew's brow furrowed. "I'm not dating any Sheryl."

Lori paused, the jelly from her knife sliding onto the English muffin's buttery surface. "It sure looked like she was your date. I mean, the woman barely let you out of her sight the entire evening."

A light dawned in his eyes. "Are you talking about *Susan?*"

"The one I'm thinking of wore a brown dress." Lori took a bite of muffin.

"That was Susan," Drew said.

"If you say so," she said. "I could have sworn her name was Sheryl."

"It doesn't matter whether her name is Susan or Sheryl," he said. "Who I date is none of your business."

"Exactly my point." Lori hid a smile. "Who you date is *your* business. Who I date is *my* business."

Drew's eyes darkened and he opened his mouth to speak.

The door to the dining room burst open.

"We're ready." Nicole entered the room dressed in a yellow sundress that was the perfect foil for her dark hair and honey-colored skin. Molly stood beside her wearing the same hot pink dress she'd worn the first time Lori had seen her.

Lori glanced down at her watch and took a hurried sip of her chai. She pushed back her chair. "We're off."

Nicole shifted her gaze to her father. "I still don't understand why we have to go and you don't."

Drew met his daughter's gaze, his expression inscrutable.

"When Mom was alive, we all went together," Nicole said.

"Things are different now," Drew said.

"You can say that again," Nicole said under her breath.

"Be sure and come right home after services," Drew said. "Susan is stopping over later and we're all going to the park for a picnic."

"I thought you told me that was next Sunday." Nicole's frown deepened. "I promised Kim and Anna I'd go shopping with them this afternoon."

"Then you'd better call and let them know you won't be able to make it," Drew said in a tone that brooked no argument.

"It's a wonder I have any friends," Nicole muttered.

Lori could empathize with the teen. But unlike Nicole, she was happy about the plans. With the girls gone, she'd have the whole afternoon to herself. If she got her column finished, she might even do some shopping.

Drew's gaze shifted to Lori. "Bring them right home."

Lori nodded. "You can count on it."

Apparently satisfied, Drew gave a slight nod and picked up the financial section of the Sunday newspaper.

Though Lori looked forward to the church service, she couldn't help but worry she'd feel out of place. But the minute she walked through the huge double doors, Lori realized there were so many parishioners, no one would know if she was a member or a guest.

"Have you been going here long?" Lori slid into the pew next to Nicole.

"Just since my mother died," Nicole said. "We used to go to Lake Forest Christian on Deerpath."

Lori had a dozen more questions on the tip of her tongue, but the service began and she didn't get a chance to ask them.

Surprisingly, the minister wasn't a very dynamic speaker. But that fact didn't excuse the girls' behavior. Shortly after the sermon started, Molly fell asleep and Nicole pulled out a Palm Pilot from her purse and proceeded to read her e-mails.

Lori nudged Molly awake and glanced pointedly at Nicole. The teen ignored her and continued scrolling through the messages.

Knowing that church was no place for a confrontation, Lori waited until they were back in the car before saying anything. "I need to talk to you two about your behavior in church today."

"What's your problem?" Nicole exchanged a glance with Molly. "We were quiet."

"That's not the point," Lori said. "I don't think either of you could tell me what the sermon was about."

"It was about God," Nicole said.

Molly nodded solemnly.

"We go to church to worship God and hear His word," Lori said. "Why even go if all you're going to do is read e-mails and sleep?"

"We go because Dad makes us," Nicole said. "The minister is boring and the other kids are snotty. At least we had friends at our old church. And Pastor Steve was funny."

Molly nodded solemnly.

"Still…" Lori said.

"Besides, Dad doesn't care if we listen to the sermon or not," Nicole said. "Ask him yourself if you don't believe me."

Lori exhaled a frustrated breath. Since she was getting nowhere with Nicole, she might just do as the teen suggested and talk to Drew.

But by the time they'd gotten home and Lori waited for the girls to go upstairs, she'd barely broached the subject when Mrs. Graham announced that Ms. Tobin had arrived.

"Send her in," Drew said to the housekeeper

before turning his attention back to Lori. "You were saying?"

"Nicole seems to think you don't care if they get anything out of the church service or not."

"I'm sorry." Susan Tobin paused in the doorway. "Mrs. Graham didn't say you were occupied. I can wait in the foyer."

Dressed in tan linen pants and a lightweight salmon-colored twin set, Susan looked more suited to an afternoon of shopping at Lord & Taylor than fighting flies at a picnic.

"Don't be silly," Drew said. "Come on in. Lori and I were just talking about the girls and church."

"Their continued relationship with God depends on them hearing His word." Lori knew she sounded preachy but she didn't know how else to get her point across. "They can't do that when they're sleeping or their mind is elsewhere. I think you should talk to them. Encourage them to—"

"I have no intention of encouraging them to listen." A tiny muscle twitched in Drew's jaw. "I'd be a hypocrite if I did."

Lori frowned, not sure if she'd heard correctly. "But you told me you wanted them to go to church. In fact you insisted."

"Their mother had a strong faith. Having them attend church was important to her," he said. "If it was up to me, they wouldn't be going."

Lori's jaw dropped open. She closed it with a snap.

"I've always believed you should let children decide for themselves if they want to go to church," Susan said.

Lori shot Susan a pointed look. She didn't remember asking the woman for her opinion. "A child needs—"

"Ladies." Drew spoke in a loud, firm tone. "I appreciate your opinions, but I'm the girls' father and it's what *I* say that matters."

"Let me make sure I've got this straight." Lori tried to hide her disappointment. "Your only requirement is that they sit in a pew every Sunday. It doesn't matter what church, or even if they get anything out of it."

"That's right," Drew said. "So we understand each other?"

"Perfectly," Lori said. If the girls were going to have a personal relationship with God, it would be up to her.

An image of Nicole's belligerent gaze flashed before her.

Lori sighed and cast her eyes heavenward. Thank goodness she wasn't in this alone.

Chapter Five

American Teen

Dear Lorelei Love,
I'm a senior in high school and I have a problem—my parents. Even though I've never given them any trouble, they don't trust me. My friend Sara's parents have a cabin at a lake and Sara has invited a bunch of us girls to spend the weekend there. My mom and dad were all for it until they found out Sara's parents weren't going to be there. Now they say absolutely not.

Is that ridiculous or what?

Not Trusted in Tulsa

Dear Not Trusted,
Hanging out at a lake with a bunch of friends sounds wonderful! When I was in high school, a group of us would do that same thing. And even though it started out as a "girls" weekend, somehow our boyfriends would always discover our plans and they'd crash the party. Of course, we didn't mind at all. Maybe one of Sara's parents would agree to stay. That way you could still have fun, but not have both of them hanging around.

LL

Drew leaned back in his favorite leather wing-back chair and let the *Sun-Times* drop to his lap.

The picnic with the girls and Susan had gone better than he'd hoped. Both Molly and Nicole had seemed to appreciate the fact that Susan didn't fawn over them. In fact, she'd focused all her attention on Drew and barely acknowledged the two girls.

It was a smart move, Drew decided. Sensing the girls' resistance, she must have decided to play it cool.

They'd spread out the food in a grassy area in full view of the lake. After a few bites, Nicole had announced she was going skating down the concrete path that followed the lake and taking Molly with her. When Drew had protested, Susan had told him to lighten up and let the girls enjoy the afternoon. Drew had reluctantly agreed.

Susan had been a pleasant companion, but during their conversation he'd found himself wondering what would have happened if he'd invited Lori to come along. Although his oldest daughter professed to disliking her new nanny, her gaze was always on Lori, and Nicole rarely left the table early when Lori dined with them. Perhaps if Lori had been with them, Nicole might have lingered longer over lunch.

As if the mere thought had conjured her up, Lori stuck her head inside the room.

"How was the picnic? Did the girls have fun?"

Drew smiled, trying not to let his relief show. When they'd returned home from the picnic and Lori wasn't around, he'd worried she was out with Tom. Not that Drew had anything against Tom, but Lori was a small-town girl and Tom was definitely a big-city guy.

"Come on in," he said. "I'll tell you all about it."

Lori crossed the room with a natural grace Drew found appealing. Taking a seat in the chair closest to his, she crossed one long leg over the other. Her skin was a warm golden hue and her legs seemed to go on forever.

He lifted his gaze and cleared his throat. "I'm surprised to see you home so early."

Lori smiled. "Tell me all about the picnic."

Drew basked in the warmth of her smile. "The weather couldn't have been better. Eighty degrees and sunny. We ate our lunch at a little spot not too far from here, just off the lake."

"That was a good idea." Lori nodded her approval. "Nicole must have liked that better than a park crawling with little kids."

"She thought it was great," Drew said. "Especially once she saw all the cute boys in the area."

"Why doesn't that surprise me?" Lori laughed. She rested her elbows on her knees. "So what did you do after you ate? Did you fly the kite Molly found in the garage?"

"There wasn't enough wind." Drew saw no reason to mention he'd forgotten to put the kite in the car. Molly had been disappointed, but Susan was right. With only a light breeze it would have taken a lot of effort to even get the thing airborne.

"So what *did* you do?" Lori's blue eyes sparkled with interest. She'd once told him that taking her brothers and sisters on frequent picnics had been one of her favorite things to do.

He shifted uneasily in his seat. "We ate and then the girls went in-line skating."

"I can't imagine Susan on Rollerblades." Lori's smile widened. "How'd she do?"

"She didn't," he said.

Lori's brows drew together in a puzzled frown. "But you said…"

"I said the girls went skating. Susan and I stayed behind."

"You let the girls go by themselves?" Lori sat up straight. "In downtown Chicago?"

"They weren't in downtown Chicago." Irritation filled Drew's tone. "I told you, we were by the lake."

"That's close enough," Lori said. "What were you thinking? They're only seven and sixteen—"

"I know very well how old they are," Drew said, keeping a tight grip on his temper. "And as their father I am the one who decides where they go and what they do."

"You're right. Molly and Nicole are your children." Lori met his gaze with an equally firm one of her own. "But they *are* children. And it's a parent's job to make sure they're protected."

For a moment all Drew could do was stare. He hadn't expected Lori to apologize. She was too stubborn for that. But he had expected her to back down. If not because she agreed, then because he was her employer.

"Don't give me that," Drew said. "I bet you gave your siblings plenty of freedom."

"Only what they could handle." She paused, as if she suddenly realized how sanctimonious she sounded. "I think, because I wasn't that much older than they were, I was more cautious than most. I knew what temptations and dangers were out there.''

''You think I don't want to keep my girls safe?'' His voice rose despite his efforts to control it.

''That's not it at all,'' Lori said in a soothing tone. ''I know you love your daughters. But from what you've said, your wife handled a lot of the day-to-day stuff. Knowing how much freedom to give a child isn't something you learn overnight.''

''You may be right,'' Drew admitted grudgingly. ''One thing I've learned in the last two years is that parenting is definitely an art, not a science.''

The understanding in Lori's gaze encouraged him to continue.

''I wanted Nicole to have a good time. When she'd said she'd thrown the Rollerblades in the trunk and asked if she and Molly could skate down the path, how could I say no?''

''Why didn't you go with her?''

''For one thing, I didn't have any Rollerblades with me.'' Drew gave a laugh. ''For another, I'm sure Nicole wouldn't be caught dead skating with her old man.''

''You'd be surprised,'' Lori said. ''Regardless of how they may act, deep down, teens want and need that closeness with their parents.''

''Where'd you learn that?'' Drew raised a brow. ''In one of your college psychology courses?''

"Actually, I did," Lori said. "And the letters I get every day from teens confirm what I learned in my course work. It's not easy growing up, especially in today's society. Kids need their parents' love and support and most of all they need their time and attention."

A knot formed in Drew's stomach. Though he'd been spending more time at home since Karen's death, had he really been giving them his attention? Even today, he'd spent more time talking to his date than he had to his daughters.

"I've always been good at most things I've tried," Drew said. "But raising children is a lot different than closing a business deal."

He remembered how easy he'd thought it would be. He and Karen had wanted a large family. They'd dreamed of filling their home with the pitter-patter of little feet. But Karen had several miscarriages and they'd been lucky to have the three children they did.

"Your children love you," Lori said softly.

"Sometimes I wonder if they need more than I can give," he said with a sigh.

"There's a cop-out if I ever heard one," Lori said with an unladylike snort.

Drew narrowed his gaze. "What do you mean by that comment?"

"You built a multimillion-dollar empire from nothing," Lori said. "I think you're more than capable of meeting the challenges of raising two girls.''

''You don't think a child needs a mother?''

''I think it's ideal for a child to have two parents that love them,'' Lori said. ''But would I recommend you rush out and marry someone just so there will be a woman in the house? Absolutely not.''

Drew stared at Lori for a long moment. She was such an enigma. On one hand she was a vivacious young woman who acted as if she didn't have a care in the world. On the other hand, raising her younger siblings had made her older than her thirty years.

He couldn't imagine her being satisfied or challenged by someone as young as Tom Bowers. Granted, Tom was a smart guy with a lot of potential, but Lori deserved a man, not a boy.

''You're so good with children,'' Drew said at last, tearing his gaze away from her lush, full lips. ''I bet you can't wait to be a mother.''

Her laugh took Drew by surprise.

''At this point in my life, being married and tied down with children is the last thing I want,'' Lori said. ''For the first time in my life, all I have to worry about is me. And that's just the way I like it.''

Lori took a sip of orange juice and wondered how she could have been so stupid.

For the first time in my life, all I have to worry about is me. And that's just the way I like it.

Lori nearly groaned out loud. The words made her sound like a child hater. No wonder Drew had been watching her so thoughtfully the past couple of days.

This morning, he'd been particularly attentive. All through breakfast, she'd felt his eyes on her. Once she'd looked up unexpectedly from buttering her pancakes and had found him staring.

To her surprise, he didn't look away. Instead his blue eyes had lingered. Though Lori rarely blushed, her cheeks had warmed even as her heart had picked up speed.

Who could blame her? She placed her juice glass on the table and studied him through lowered lashes. Today he was wearing a shirt that was one of her favorites, a navy cotton that made his eyes as blue as the ocean depths. And his hair, still damp from the shower, curled just above his ears. She resisted a crazy urge to lean across the table and run her fingers through the auburn curls.

"Mr. McCashlin." Mrs. Graham stood in the doorway. "Mrs. Barrett just called. She said to tell you she'll be here in fifteen minutes to pick up the girls."

A bright smile flashed across Nicole's face. "Is that today?"

Drew groaned. He'd completely forgotten Celia was coming.

"Who's Mrs. Barrett?" Lori asked, looking at Drew.

To Lori's surprise, Nicole answered. "She's our grandmother. My mother's mother. She's cool."

Lori lifted a brow. Coming from Nicole, the words were high praise indeed.

Molly nodded in agreement, her blue eyes dancing.

Drew's gaze shifted to Nicole. "But weren't you going to Great America today with your friends?"

"I'd rather go shopping with Gram," Nicole said.

"I can make Molly's excuses to her friends," Lori said.

"Gram will be disappointed if we can't go," Nicole added, as if suddenly afraid her dad was going to say no.

"You bet I'd be disappointed." A woman's voice sounded from the doorway.

"Gram." Nicole smiled in welcome.

Lori turned in her chair. The slender dark-haired woman was dressed casually in a pair of lemon-colored linen pants and a matching jacket. Though she had to be close to retirement age, the woman Nicole called "Gram" radiated a youthful vitality.

Molly jumped to her feet and ran to her grandmother's arms.

"Now what's this nonsense about your not being able to go today?"

"Dad had the dates mixed up," Nicole said, casting a sideways glance at her father.

"Drew." Reproach filled the woman's voice. "I've been looking forward to spending the day with the girls all week."

"I never said they couldn't go, Celia," Drew said with an easy smile. "Nicole just needs to let her friends know there's been a change of plans."

Nicole pushed back her chair and stood. "I'll call them now."

Lori smiled at the excitement on the teen's face and watched Nicole leave the room. When she shifted her attention back to Celia, she found the woman staring with unabashed interest.

Mrs. Barrett's lips curved in a smile. She crossed the room and extended her hand to Lori. "I'm Celia Barrett. But my friends call me CeCe."

Lori stood, liking the woman's direct gaze and firm handshake.

"I'm Lorelei Loveland, the new nanny. But you can call me Lori."

"Lorelei Loveland." Celia raised a brow. "That's an interesting name. Sounds like a—"

"Advice columnist," Drew said suddenly, flashing Lori a smile. "Lori writes an advice column for *American Teen* magazine called 'Ask Lorelei Love.'"

"'Ask Lorelei Love'?" Celia rolled the words on her tongue then nodded. "I like it. Catchy."

"That's what the editor thought," Lori said with a wry smile. "Personally I think it makes me sound like a stripper."

Drew choked on his coffee.

"You may be right." Celia laughed. "But it *is* cute."

"The column has been very successful." Lori joined in the woman's laughter. "So I guess I'll have to agree."

"What kind of things do teens write to you about?" Celia's eyes were bright with interest.

Lori could see why her grandchildren adored her. The woman radiated an exciting energy.

"It runs the gamut," Lori said, "from problems at school or home to relationship issues."

"You must like teenagers." Celia's hazel eyes grew thoughtful.

"I do." Lori smiled. "They're so intense, so full of life."

"I bet you're good at what you do," Celia said.

Lori flushed with pleasure. "I do my best."

Nicole entered the room, her black leather backpack slung over one shoulder. "Ready to go, Gram?"

"In a minute, honey." Celia smiled at her granddaughter. "Lori and I were just talking about her other job."

"Gram—" Nicole heaved an exasperated sigh "—I'm sure the nanny has work to do."

Drew frowned, but Lori shook her head slightly. Nicole's attitude didn't surprise her. Though most of the time Nicole was civil, she'd never been interested in Lori's personal life.

When Lori had tried to talk to Nicole about her advice column, the girl had always cut her off before she could begin.

"I'll have them back by ten." Celia smiled, shifting her gaze to Drew. "If that's not too late."

"That'll be just fine."

But once the girls and their grandmother had left, Drew leaned back in his chair. "It figures that the one night I'd planned to be home by five, the girls would be gone."

"You hadn't mentioned coming home early," Lori said.

Drew took a sip of coffee and smiled ruefully. "It was going to be a surprise. I'd even made reservations at Teddy R's, that new place downtown."

"I think Tom told me about that place," Lori said. "Isn't that the one that has live jazz?"

Drew nodded. "And every Tuesday is family night. Nicole and Molly both like jazz."

"So do I," Lori said. "Unfortunately I haven't got to see many artists in person. Not a lot of jazz musicians stopped in Shelby."

Drew gazed thoughtfully at Lori. It would be a shame to waste the reservations. Susan hated jazz with a passion, so it would be pointless to call her.

He could ask Lori to go with him.

But I'm dating Susan.

Drew shoved the thought aside. Though he and Susan had gone out five or six times in the past couple of months, they'd never talked about being exclusive. Anyway, this wouldn't be a date. It would just be two people who appreciated jazz going out together.

His gaze returned to Lori. To her silvery blond hair and big blue eyes. To her full pouty lips.

No, it wouldn't be a date. Not at all.

Chapter Six

American Teen

Dear Lorelei Love,
Have you ever been so crazy about a guy, you can hardly stand it, then he kisses you and you get scared?

I had liked this guy at my school forever, but he'd never really noticed me until we became counselors at the same day camp. Last night he kissed me for the first time. It was so wonderful! Better than anything I'd ever imagined.

But now I'm scared. What if it doesn't last? What if when we go back to school he ignores me? What if he thinks I don't kiss very well and tells his friends?

Regrets in Rhode Island

Dear Regrets,
Chances are if you enjoyed the kiss, so did
he! I would just caution you to take it slow.
Take time to get to know him better and you
won't have to wonder what he's thinking because you'll already know.

                                        LL

Though Lori didn't consider herself an expert on
good-versus-bad seating, even she could tell that
their table, tucked off to the side in a tiny alcove,
was one of Teddy R's best. It had a great view of
the stage but enough privacy to give an aura of
intimacy.

Lori glanced around, a tingle of excitement trav-
eling up her spine. If she'd stayed in Shelby, she'd
probably be having a burger at the Shelby Lanes'
snack bar right now. Instead, she was out on the
town in one of the country's largest cities. And
accompanied by a man who looked like he'd just
stepped off the pages of *GQ*.

Though Drew had told her to dress casually,
he'd worn a coat and tie. The tie he'd chosen made
his eyes look as blue as the sky on a clear summer
day.

Lori's heart picked up speed.

"I like your tie," she said.

Drew looked up from the menu and smiled. "Clay gave it to me for my last birthday."

"He must have known it would go great with your eyes." The words popped out before Lori could stop them.

"Somehow I don't think that thought entered his mind." Drew's smile widened. "The truth is, my son loves Valentino ties and he thinks everyone should have at least one."

Lori leaned forward and slid the tie between her thumb and forefinger. "It *is* as soft as it looks."

"I imagine it is," Drew said softly.

She lifted her eyes and met his gaze. Her heart skipped a beat.

He lifted his hand and gently brushed back a strand of her hair, letting it fall between his fingers.

"Incredibly soft," Drew said in a low voice, his eyes never leaving hers. His hand cupped her face.

Anticipation coursed up her spine. Her lips parted slightly.

"Drew McCashlin? Is that you?" The raspy male voice was like a splash of cold water.

Lori jumped.

Drew's hand dropped to his side and, with a composure Lori couldn't help but envy, he rose to face the short portly man who'd stopped next to the table. "Bob. What a surprise."

Bob smiled. The man had to be close to fifty and what hair he still had was peppered with gray.

The woman at his side was about the same age, only she had thick chestnut-colored hair. Like her companion, her smile was friendly.

"I'm not sure if you remember my wife, Marge?" Bob asked Drew.

"Of course I do." Drew directed a warm smile in the woman's direction. "How nice to see you again."

"It's nice to see you, too, Mr. McCashlin."

"Please—" Drew smiled and the little dimple flashed in his cheek "—call me Drew."

Marge's plump cheeks turned pink and Lori couldn't help but smile. When Drew turned on the charm, he was hard to resist.

Bob's gaze shifted to Lori and Drew followed his gaze.

"I'd like to introduce Lorelei Loveland, a friend of mine. Lori is new to Chicago. Lori, Bob and Marge Henderson. Bob is a key member of our accounting team."

"Pleased to meet you both." Though they seemed like a nice couple, Lori crossed her fingers that the two wouldn't end up joining them.

If they did, Lori could already predict the way the conversation would go. Marge would bring up children and would spend most of the meal discussing soccer and proms. Bob would mention some work-related issue, and while the two men talked, Marge would pump Lori for information.

And no matter what she said, Lori knew Marge wouldn't believe she and Drew were just friends.

"Would you two like to join us?" Drew gestured to the empty chairs at the table.

Lori held her breath.

"I wish we could." Regret blanketed Bob's face. "But Marge's brother and his wife are joining us this evening."

Lori released the breath she'd been holding. "That's too bad."

"Another time, perhaps," Drew said.

Lori smiled goodbye and watched them weave their way across the crowded restaurant. When they took a seat at a table toward the back, Lori turned her attention back to Drew. "It's too bad they couldn't join us."

Drew laughed. "I'm glad they said no, too."

Lori tilted her head. "You were?"

He nodded. "I wanted you to have a nice time. Talking about kids and work all evening wouldn't be much fun."

Lori groaned. "Was I that transparent?"

Drew patted her hand reassuringly. "Don't worry. They didn't notice a thing. The only reason I knew was because I was thinking the same thing."

"Really?" Lori grinned. "Now that's a scary thought."

"What is?"

"You and I. On the same wavelength." Lori saw the waiter approaching and lowered her voice to a conspiratorial whisper. "I mean, if you know what I'm thinking, then you must know I want—"

"This?" Unexpectedly Drew leaned across the table and brushed her mouth with his. The touch of his lips took her breath away.

Lori hid a smile. And to think she was going to suggest a glass of wine.

"Have you decided what you want?" The waiter stood at tableside, pencil poised.

Drew smiled at Lori. "I know just what I want."

Lori leaned her head back against the truck's leather seats and heaved a happy sigh. It had been a wonderful evening.

She and Drew had talked all through dinner. They'd discussed so many topics, she couldn't remember half of them. After the first jazz set, they'd decided to stay and have dessert. By the time they'd finished their créme brûlée, the second set had started, so Drew had ordered some cognac and they'd sat back and let the music wash over them.

When the waiter had brought their bill, Lori had automatically reached for her bag, expecting to pay her half. Drew wouldn't hear of it. His jaw had set

in a stubborn tilt and Lori knew it would be pointless to argue.

By the time the waiter had brought back Drew's
credit card, Lori's eyelids had started to droop.

"I can't believe I'm so tired," Lori said, almost
to herself.

"You were up early," Drew said with an understanding smile. "And it *is* almost midnight."

"Midnight?" Lori sat up straight in the seat.
"Wasn't your mother-in-law going to have the
girls home by ten?"

"That's all taken care of," Drew said. "I
warned Mrs. Graham we might be late. She promised to be available."

"You thought of everything, didn't you?" Lori
said, admiration evident in her tone. She'd always
liked a take-charge attitude.

"You found me out," he said with a sheepish
grin. "I tend to be a planner, except..."

"Except?" Lori echoed.

"I didn't plan to kiss you tonight," he admitted.

"That's okay," Lori said with an impish smile.
"We all need a little spontaneity in our life."

"You're not offended?"

"Why would I be offended?"

"I'm your boss," he said.

"At that particular moment, you didn't seem
like my boss," she said. "So I think we're okay."

Relief filled Drew's gaze. "I had a great evening."

"I did, too." Though Lori spoke automatically, she realized the words were true. It had been a long time since she'd enjoyed an evening more.

Oh, she'd had fun with Tom, and she was definitely looking forward to seeing him again. But with Tom she had to play the dating game. Because there was no romantic involvement with Drew, there were no games, and she could just be herself.

She could talk to Drew about her sister wanting to get her tongue pierced, without his eyes glazing over. Because he had a teenage daughter, he understood her concerns. When she'd mentioned it to Tom, he'd just shrugged and asked why she was getting all uptight. After all, it wasn't her tongue.

She could understand Tom's reaction. How could he be expected to know how a parent felt, when he'd never been in that situation? But she vowed not to mention her siblings again. After all, part of the reason for moving to Chicago was to live her own life.

Lori and Drew rode home in comfortable silence. By the time the truck was parked in the garage and they'd entered the quiet house, the cognac had relaxed every tense muscle in Lori's body.

"Good night." Drew extended his hand.

Lori made no move to take his hand. Her gaze

met his. "You forget. We're on the same wavelength. A handshake isn't the way either of us wants to end the night."

Without giving a second thought to the wisdom of her action, Lori took a step forward and wrapped her arms around his neck.

His eyes darkened. "Are you sure?"

The spicy scent of his cologne closed in around her and her senses whirled. Her heart pounded in her chest.

"There's nothing wrong with a good-night kiss between friends." Lori lowered one hand and played with his tie. "And if we don't do it, I have the feeling neither one of us will be able to sleep tonight."

A muscle twitched in Drew's jaw. "I'd say we don't have much choice."

"I don't think we do."

It was all the invitation Drew needed. Using his right hand, Drew pushed her hair back from her face. He bent down and brushed her lips with his own, much as he had in the restaurant.

But this time it wasn't enough. Lori could feel her heart beating heavily and she struggled to keep her breathing steady. "Is that all?"

Drew kissed her again, longer this time, letting his mouth linger. It was still as sweet, still as gentle.

Though she wanted nothing more than to lace

her fingers through his thick, dark hair and see if she could shatter his tightly held control, Lori just smiled.

"Good night." She turned and started up the stairs. But after a couple of steps, she stopped and turned back to Drew. "I had a wonderful time."

"I did, too." His gaze met hers. "Maybe we can do it again sometime."

And because they were on the same wavelength, Lori knew he not only wanted to take her out, he also wanted to kiss her again. He wasn't the man she was looking for, but she did like him.

"Sure." Lori smiled. "Any time."

The moment Lori turned back to the stairs, Nicole scampered down the hall and slipped inside her room. She pulled the door closed and leaned against it.

Hot anger coursed through her veins. What had her father been thinking? The woman was the *nanny*, a *servant*.

A hard knot formed in Nicole's stomach. When Gram had dropped her and Molly off, Nicole had expected her dad to be home waiting. But instead, Mrs. Graham had informed them that their father had gone out for the evening.

Nicole had noticed that Lori wasn't around, but Nicole had never once considered that her father and the nanny were out *together*. After all, her father was dating Susan. And Lori was seeing Tom Bowers.

Of course, Tom Bowers wasn't nearly as rich, or as handsome, as her father. Though Nicole didn't know Tom well, Clay had once told her his friend was a smart guy. He'd probably taken the nanny out a couple of times and seen right through those big blue eyes.

Unfortunately her dad hadn't much experience with women. If only she knew the best way to proceed. It wouldn't do to confront her dad. He'd just tell her it was none of her business. And Molly was too young to be of any help.

Nicole crossed the room and plopped down on the bed, her mind racing. Who did she know who had experience in these kinds of matters?

Erin.

Her friend had single-handedly broken up her mother's romance with their pool boy last year. She should have some good suggestions.

Nicole glanced at the clock. It was almost twelve-thirty so it would be almost one-thirty in Massachusetts. Though it might be a little late to call, Erin would understand once she explained the circumstances.

Nicole punched in the speed-dial number. Erin answered on the fourth ring.

"Erin, it's Nicole."

"Nicole?" Erin's voice was thick with sleep. "What time is it?"

"That doesn't matter," Nicole said. "I need your help."

"What's up?"

Nicole hesitated. It was embarrassing to admit her father was behaving so foolishly. But if anyone would understand, it would be Erin.

"Remember your mother and that Ryan character?"

"The pool boy?" Erin snorted. "How could I forget? I was the one who found the two of them together in the cabana."

"Well, tonight…" Nicole paused, finding the words difficult to say. "Tonight, I saw my father with the nanny."

"No way!"

"Way," Nicole said.

"Let me get this straight." All sleepiness had vanished from Erin's voice. "You caught your dad in bed with your nanny?"

"She's not *my* nanny. She's Molly's nanny," Nicole clarified. "And they're not having an affair. Not yet anyway. But I did see him kissing her."

"And she's good-looking, right?"

Nicole thought of Lori's long blond hair, big blue eyes and shapely curves. "Guys seem to think so."

"What is it with them anyway?" Erin's voice

filled with disgust. "It's almost as if they get to a certain age and they have to revisit their childhood."

"I don't know," Nicole said. "But I don't want this to get out of control."

"Isn't he still dating Susan Tobin?"

"Off and on," Nicole said. "At least she's his age."

"And more the same class," Erin said, voicing Nicole's own thoughts. "Your nanny is probably trying to snag herself a rich man."

"But he's got two kids at home," Nicole said. "She's young. Why would she want a guy when he comes with baggage?"

"Hel-lo," Erin said. "He also comes with millions of dollars. And she could always pack you and your sister off to boarding school."

A shiver traveled down Nicole's spine. Even though she wouldn't want to go away to school, if it happened, she'd survive. But Molly needed familiar surroundings, if there was any hope of her ever talking again. "My dad would never allow that to happen."

"Are you sure?"

Nicole paused. She wanted to say she was sure. The trouble was she wasn't sure.

Not at all.

It had been ridiculous, Drew decided, to skip breakfast the past two mornings in order to avoid

Lori. After all, it was no big deal. They'd kissed a few times. So what?

This morning he'd decided the foolishness would end. And so far everything had gone smoothly. Drew took a sip of his coffee and glanced across the table. Though the simple sundress Lori had on did nothing to enhance her ample curves, Drew swore she'd never looked prettier.

"I like your dress," he said.

"Thank you. Tom and I are going shopping this afternoon."

"Shopping?" Drew raised a brow. "He likes to *shop?*"

Lori laughed. "I don't know if he likes to, but this is a necessity thing. He rented a three-flat over in Lincoln Park and he needs furniture."

Drew tightened his grip on his cup. "I thought he was staying with his parents."

Lori laughed. "I think he found his parents' home somewhat confining."

"I don't know why," Drew said. "They have a big house. I'm sure they—"

"Drew," Lori interrupted. "It's not our decision. It's his."

"Are you two still dating?" Nicole, who'd been silent since she'd sat down, suddenly spoke up.

Lori's eyes widened. "Who told you I was dating Tom?"

Nicole shrugged. "Everybody knows he took you to his parents' party. Now you're going shopping for furniture. Are you going to move in with him?"

"Nicole Marie McCashlin." Drew shot his daughter a leveling glance. "What kind of question is that?"

"People live together all the time," Nicole said.

"Unfortunately that's true," Lori said, an easy smile on her face. "But that doesn't make it right."

The tension in Drew's stomach eased.

"So does that mean no?" Like a dog with a bone, Nicole persisted.

"That's exactly what it means," Lori said matter-of-factly, taking a bite of grapefruit.

"But you two *are* still dating, right?" An odd hint of desperation ran through Nicole's tone.

Lori shrugged. "We went to that party. And now we're going shopping. So if you consider that dating, I guess we're dating."

"Do you kiss on a first date?" Nicole asked.

"Why do you want to know?"

To Drew's surprise, Lori didn't seem offended by the question, just curious. Then he remembered her advice column and realized she probably discussed these issues—and more—in her column.

Though he didn't appreciate Nicole putting Lori on the spot, he wondered if this might be a positive sign. Perhaps Nicole was finally starting to accept Lori.

"My friends and I were talking and some of us thought it was sleazy to kiss a guy on a first date," Nicole said. "That it makes you look easy."

Drew took a sip of coffee and resisted the urge to glance in Lori's direction. If he didn't know better, he'd think that Nicole knew he and Lori had kissed. But thankfully she'd been asleep when they'd gotten home.

Lori was quiet for a moment. "I guess I'd say it depends. On how long you've known the guy, how well you know him. On what type of kiss."

"Did you kiss Tom on your first date?"

Drew knew he should step in, and from the look Lori shot him he knew she expected him to, but he kept silent. It wasn't only his daughter who was curious about the answer to that question.

Lori paused for a long moment. "Yes, I kissed him."

Nicole's lips turned up in a pleased smile.

The knot in Drew's stomach tightened, even though he told himself he'd known all along the kisses he and Lori had shared hadn't meant a thing.

"By the way, Dad, did I tell you Angie McCade is going to Miss Porter's next year?" Nicole asked in a casual tone.

Drew seized the opportunity to change the subject. "Isn't that a boarding school back East?"

Nicole nodded.

"That surprises me," Drew said. "Why is she going away?"

After Karen had died, some well-meaning friends had given him names of several good boarding schools and suggested that he might want to look into them for Molly and Nicole. But he hadn't made a single call. He didn't want the girls living away from home when they were young. There would be time enough for that when they were in college.

"Her parents split up last year," Nicole said. "Her mother has a new boyfriend now."

"That has to be hard," Lori murmured.

"What's hard? Having a sixteen-year-old daughter hanging around?"

"I was referring to living away from home." Lori met Nicole's gaze. "But at least Miss Porter's has a good reputation."

Drew wondered if Lori remembered their conversation the other night, when he'd mentioned he worried Nicole might be reluctant to go away to college.

"And boarding school is almost like living in the dorm at college," Drew said. "Angie will probably love it."

"Yeah, right." Nicole's gaze shifted to Lori. "Would you ever send a child away to boarding school?"

"That depends," Lori said, finishing the last of her grapefruit.

"On what?" Nicole asked.

Lori was silent for a moment. "On the school. On if I had the money. On if the child wanted to go."

Nicole leaned forward, resting her arms on the table. "What if the child didn't want to go? Angie doesn't want to go, but—"

"Nicole, that's enough," Drew said. "Angie is a child. Her parents are doing what they think is best."

Nicole's gaze met his, and for a second Drew could have sworn he saw disappointment in her eyes. But that was crazy. All he wanted was the best for his girls. And Nicole had to know that.

Chapter Seven

American Teen

Dear Lorelei Love,
Someone from school told everyone they'd
seen me shoplift a CD at the mall. It's not
true. I would never steal. What really bothers
me, though, is my best friend believed I'd
done it. And, to make it worse, the fact that
I could be a thief didn't even bother her! Am
I wrong to feel hurt?

Hurtin' in Huntsville

Dear Hurtin',
I can see why you'd be bummed. Your friend
thinks you're a thief. It makes me wonder
how well you two really know each other.

Maybe the next time you're together try to talk to her about something more than clothes and boys. That way she can get to know you better and hopefully understand you'd never steal.

LL

"Are you sure you don't want to stop over and see my place?" Tom trailed a finger up Lori's bare arm.

Lori stared into his hazel eyes, not the least bit fooled by the innocence she found there. They'd spent the afternoon wandering through furniture stores until Tom had finally found what he wanted at the Eddie Bauer store on Michigan Avenue. After he'd completed the order, they'd stopped at a nearby coffee shop for a latte.

Though up to this point the conversation had concerned furniture, Lori knew by the way Tom's gaze lingered on her lips that he now had other things on his mind.

She smiled and pulled her hand out from beneath his on the pretext of brushing a strand of hair back from her face.

"It's not that I don't *want* to see it," Lori explained, regret coloring her tone. "But I have plans for this evening."

She didn't, of course, have any plans beyond working on her latest column. But Tom didn't need to know that. After all, when he'd called on Wednesday, he'd specifically asked her to spend Friday *afternoon* with him. If he'd wanted to go out with her in the evening, he should have asked then.

Tom lifted the cup to his lip and took a long sip. "Do these plans include Drew McCashlin?"

"Drew?" Lori's brows furrowed into a frown. "What does he have to do with anything?"

Tom laughed. "I saw the way he looked at you at my parents' party."

Lori rolled her eyes. "Whatever."

"He likes you," Tom said. "And not just as a friend."

"Yeah, right."

"Don't even try to tell me you can't see it." Tom set his cup down and leaned back in his chair. He studied Lori for a long moment. "He's been without a woman for a long time. And now he has a beautiful one under the same roof...."

"You're forgetting two important facts," Lori said. "First, Drew has a girlfriend. Second, I'm his employee."

"Susan Tobin is an ice queen," Tom said. "And as far as you working for him, that little detail never stopped any man."

Tom's words rankled. He made it sound as if Drew was a predator and she was his prey. Actually, nothing could be further from the truth.

She'd never been a helpless rabbit, and Drew was anything but a marauding lion. What kisses they had shared had been sweet and gentle.

Designed, perhaps, to soften me up? To get me to lower my resistance?

Lori shoved the thought aside. Drew was an honorable man and she wasn't about to let Tom's vivid imagination change her opinion.

"You found me out," Lori said with a laugh. "Drew and I are having this torrid love affair, but don't tell any—"

"Nicole," Tom interrupted, casting Lori a warning glance. "Haven't seen you in a while."

Lori's breath caught in her throat. She turned slowly in her seat, praying that the Nicole whom Tom had greeted was anyone but the Nicole she knew.

Her heart skipped a beat at the sight of the slender dark-haired girl.

"Well, if it isn't the nanny." Nicole's steely-eyed gaze settled momentarily on Lori.

Lori forced a smile and nodded a greeting to Nicole's companions before turning her attention back to Nicole. "Your father didn't tell me you were going shopping this afternoon."

"You're the help." Nicole spoke in a condescending arrogant tone. "I'm sure he tells you only what you need to know."

Nicole shifted her gaze to Tom, effectively dismissing Lori. "You'll have to stop by the house sometime. I've missed seeing you around."

If Lori didn't know better, she'd have thought Nicole was flirting with Tom. And if she didn't know better, she'd think he was enjoying it.

His smile had widened to include Nicole and her two girlfriends. "I just may have to do that."

Lori had to admit the three were an engaging sight with their long tan legs and curvy figures. Though they were only sixteen, any one of them could have easily passed for a college student. But they weren't in college. They were in high school. And Tom needed to remember that fact.

"Nicole." The tall blonde glanced impatiently at her watch. "We don't have much time if we're going to make the movie."

"Gotta go." Nicole wiggled her fingers and smiled at Tom. "See you around."

The girl ignored Lori's goodbye, and turned on her heel, heading to the counter to order.

Lori waited until Nicole was out of earshot before she spoke. "Do you think she heard what I said?"

Tom pulled his gaze from the girls. "You mean about you and Drew having an affair?"

Lori nodded.

"If I had to guess," he said, "I'd say yes. She was right behind you when I first saw her and your voice has a tendency to carry."

Lori closed her eyes for a brief second. Dear God, could it get much worse?

"Hey—" Tom touched her arm "—it's no big deal. She'd have found out soon enough about you and her dad—"

"There's nothing to find out," Lori said in a furious tone, remembering at the last minute to lower her voice. She couldn't believe her ears. She'd only been joking, telling Tom by her ridiculous response how far off base he was with his suspicions. But Nicole wouldn't know that. She might think Lori was serious.

Lori leaned across the table, not wanting to speak any louder than absolutely necessary. "There's *nothing* going on between Drew McCashlin and me."

Tom's gaze searched hers.

"I'm not sure I believe you," he said finally. "And if I don't believe you, I'm sure Nicole won't."

Lori stared, dumbfounded. "You actually think I'm sleeping with my boss?"

"Don't get defensive. He's attracted to you. I can understand that." Tom's gaze lingered on her face. "Because I feel the same way."

"But even if I would concede that Drew is attracted to me, it takes two for—"

Tom raised one hand. "If you're going to say

he's just your employer, save your breath. I can tell you right now I don't buy it."

"Okay, so I think he's attractive, not to mention he's got tons of money. But he's also got two kids. And—"

"See ya, Tom." Nicole stood at the tableside, a tall to-go cup in her hand.

"Be good," Tom said, giving the girl a rakish wink. His gaze followed the three young women out the door. "That Nicole is going to be one good-looking woman when she grows up."

"But right now she's just a little girl," Lori said. "A little girl who thinks I'm having an affair with her father."

"It could be worse," Tom said, finishing off the last of his latte. "She could think you want to marry him."

After returning from her shopping trip with Tom, Lori spent the evening in her room working on her column. The problems of her readers helped keep her mind off of Nicole. And Drew. And Tom.

She pushed back her chair from the desk and rubbed the back of her neck with one hand. The afternoon couldn't have gone worse.

How could Tom have believed she was capable of having a casual affair with her employer? Though she and Tom hadn't specifically discussed values, he knew she went to church and was a

Christian. Plus she had said enough that he should have known she didn't believe in premarital sex, not to mention sleeping with one man while dating another.

What was really amazing was the fact that the thought of her sleeping with Drew hadn't even seemed to bother him.

Lori heaved a heavy sigh, glad that Nicole had decided to spend the night with friends and that Drew had a meeting.

She had some serious thinking to do and it would be easier without distractions. Thankfully, she'd always found stormy weather conducive to meditation.

Rain pelted the windowpanes and thunder rumbled in the darkened sky. But the light from the bedside lamp gave the room a mellow glow. Dressed in a pair of sweatpants and a T-shirt, with her hair pulled back in a loose braid, Lori couldn't have been more comfortable. The only thing missing was a nice cup of hot cocoa.

Sliding her feet into her bear-claw slippers, she headed for the kitchen. She'd barely made it to the edge of the stairs when a crack of lightning split the air. Seconds later a loud boom shook the entire house.

If Lori hadn't paused to adjust her slippers, she might have missed the cry. Though the sound didn't repeat, Lori frowned, certain it had come from Molly's room.

She moved quickly to the door, rapping her knuckles against the heavy wood. "Molly, are you okay?"

Lori waited for a few seconds before knocking again, harder this time. "Molly. It's Lori."

Her brows drew together. Mrs. Graham had told her Molly was watching a movie in her room. Lori moved closer and placed her ear against the door. Though television noise filled the room, Lori swore she could hear crying.

Lori didn't think twice. She reached for the doorknob and heaved a sigh of relief when it turned easily. The moment she stepped inside the open doorway, her gaze scanned the room.

The television was on, but Molly wasn't watching it. Instead the little girl sat huddled in a corner chair, her knees up against her chest and her arms around her legs. Tears streamed down the child's face.

"Molly, honey." Lori hurried across the room. She knelt at the little girl's side. "Sweetheart, what's wrong?"

At that moment another loud crack rent the air and Molly jumped, her face white as a ghost. Suddenly Lori remembered Drew mentioning Molly had been afraid of thunder since the car accident.

Apparently the accident that had claimed her mother's life had happened during a downpour.

Lori wrapped her arms around the little girl, murmuring words of comfort. Thankfully, Molly didn't pull away.

It took a long time for Molly's trembling to stop. But Lori didn't care. She held Molly in her lap and stroked her hair, just as she'd done for her brothers and sisters when they'd been frightened.

After a while the thunder moved off into the distance and the rain turned to a gentle pitter-patter against the rooftop. But Lori continued to hum songs from her childhood and hold Molly close.

Until the rain ceased entirely.

Until the child fell asleep in her arms.

Until Lori's own lids grew so heavy she could keep them open no longer.

Drew tossed his briefcase on the side table in the foyer and headed up to his daughter's room, taking the steps two at a time.

He'd been meeting with a group of his top-level managers when he'd heard the first rumble of thunder. Immediately Molly's face flashed before him. A knot formed in the pit of his stomach at the thought of his daughter being scared and home without him.

Drew had quickly ended the meeting. As he'd driven home, he could only hope the thunderstorm that had rumbled through the downtown area had bypassed Evanston.

Reaching the top of the stairs, Drew noticed Molly's door ajar. He shoved the door open, his heart pounding in his chest.

"Mol—" The words died in his throat the moment he saw her cradled in Lori's arms in the oversize chair...fast asleep.

The tear tracks on his daughter's cheeks told Drew that the storm hadn't missed Evanston, but Lori's presence told him his daughter hadn't been alone in her room. Though he hadn't had much use for God since Karen died, Drew offered up a prayer of thanks.

He stood there for a long moment, a bittersweet ache in his heart. His gaze shifted to Lori, moving from the wisps of hair that had come loose from her braid and curled against her cheek, to the ridiculous slippers on her feet.

She looked like an angel sitting there, with his daughter in her arms. While he was staring, her lids fluttered open.

"Drew?" She blinked and he could see her trying to remember where she was.

"Shh." He touched his fingers to his lips and glanced pointedly at Molly.

Lori looked down and a sweet tenderness crossed her face. "She was scared."

He nodded and crossed the room, stopping at

Molly's bed to pull back the covers, before moving to the chair.

"Let me take her." He lifted the sleeping girl into his arms and carried her to the bed, tucking her gently beneath the covers.

"Come on," he whispered to Lori. "She'll be fine now."

Lori cast one more glance at Molly before crossing the room and exiting through the door Drew held open.

Once the door was shut, Drew turned to Lori. "I know you had the night off. But I can't tell you how much I appreciate your being there for her."

"She was really scared," Lori said.

"I know," he said, raking a hand through his hair. For the hundredth time that night Drew regretted the fact that he hadn't been there for his daughter. "She shouldn't have been alone."

"But she wasn't alone," Lori said reassuringly as if she could feel his guilt. "I was with her."

"I should have been here," he said. "If I had known there was even a chance of thunderstorms…"

"It's okay." Lori laid a hand on his arm.

"It's not okay." Drew wiped a weary hand across his face. "She's my daughter. She needed me. I should have been there for her."

But instead, where had he been? At work. Leaving someone else to pick up the slack. *Again.*

"You're here now and that's what matters," Lori said matter-of-factly. Her gaze narrowed. "You look like you could use a drink."

"I think you're right," Drew said, raising a hand to massage his tight neck muscles. "I have some bourbon in the cabinet—"

"I was thinking more along the lines of hot cocoa," Lori said with an impish grin. "Why don't you get out of that suit and put on something more comfortable and I'll start warming the milk?"

"You don't have to go to all of that trouble," Drew protested. "I'm sure Mrs. Graham has some instant stuff in the cupboard."

"And that's just where it's going to stay." Lori spoke with surprising firmness. "I want the real thing. Not a cheap imitation."

She looked so serious Drew had to laugh.

"Okay," he said. "The real thing it is."

As he headed to his bedroom for a change of clothes, Drew realized the fatigue and tension that had gripped him only moments before had vanished.

And hot cocoa had never sounded so good.

It was almost eleven by the time Drew and Lori drained the last of the sweet chocolate from their cups. Though the warm milk should have made him sleepy, Drew felt anything but tired. Instead a curious tension surged through his body. From the moment he and Lori had sat down at the kitchen table, the air surrounding them had been filled with a strange electricity. Drew had tried to ignore it, but the more he tried, the more conscious he was of Lori's closeness; of her luscious full lips, the scintillating smell of her perfume.

That's why when Lori said it was time for her to get to bed, he didn't try to stop her. And he didn't offer to join her. Because in some ways he was glad to see her go. If she stayed much longer he wasn't sure what he might do. Or say. This overwhelming attraction toward a woman, other than his wife, was a new experience.

When he'd started dating Susan, it hadn't taken him long to realize that though he enjoyed her company, he didn't desire her. But with Lori it was different. When he was with her he felt sixteen again. That's why he'd let her go upstairs without saying another word or making a single move.

Because in spite of his attraction, Drew had never been a guy who acted on impulse. And he wasn't about to start now.

Chapter Eight

American Teen

Dear Lorelei Love,
My best friend is a guy. Lately he's been saying little things that make me think he wants us to be more than friends. But even though he's a lot of fun and I love him to death, I can't imagine kissing him! My girl-friend says maybe that attraction will build over time. But he's been my friend for two years and it's still not there.

Confused in Cleveland

Dear Confused,
Although love can grow over time, I think in your case if it's not there by now, it's not

going to be. You can't make yourself love someone. If your guy friend asks you out, stand firm and tell him you want to just be friends. In the long run, it will be the best thing for your friendship.

LL

Lori stifled a yawn as she pulled into the church parking lot and shut off the engine. "We're a few minutes early. You girls should have time to talk to your friends before the service begins."

"My dad's going to be mad we came here." Nicole slanted a sideways glance, speaking to Lori for the first time since they'd left home.

Lori cast aside her own misgivings, reminding herself that Drew hadn't specifically said she couldn't take the girls back to their old church.

"Your father said he wanted you in church on Sunday." Lori shifted her gaze to the white clapboard structure with the picturesque steeple. "I'd say this qualifies."

"Molly!" A little girl with long dark pigtails knocked on the window, an excited smile on her face.

Molly's face lit up and she unbuckled her seat belt, eagerly pushing open the car door.

"That's Amy." Nicole flipped down the vanity mirror and applied some lip gloss. "Her dad works for mine. He'll probably tell him he saw us."

Lori ignored the veiled warning and reached for the door handle. "Shall we go in?"

"We might as well," Nicole said with a sigh, flicking the mirror shut. "The sooner we get started, the sooner it'll be over."

Nicole walked toward the door with long, purposeful strides, leaving Lori no choice but to follow behind. But despite the teen's self-assured demeanor, Lori had the feeling the girl was nowhere near as confident as she appeared.

Once inside the tiny church, the tense set to Nicole's shoulders eased somewhat as several friends stopped to greet her. The only awkward moment came when Lori heard one of the girls ask Nicole if Lori was her stepmom.

"Are you kidding?" Nicole replied with a derisive glance in Lori's direction. "She's Molly's nanny."

Lori merely smiled, thankful it was time to find a seat.

After the opening hymn, the minister asked the young parishioners to come forward for the "Children's Sermon." Lori couldn't hide her surprise when Molly stood and headed to the front. Amy joined her halfway down the aisle. Out of the corner of her eye, Lori could see Nicole's expression. Apparently Lori wasn't the only one surprised at Molly's boldness.

After the service, Lori stood outside in the warm

sunshine and let the girls visit with their friends. Molly was surrounded by a group of little girls. And Nicole, for all her earlier talk, seemed in no hurry to leave. Especially not after she saw Justin Walker, the boy she'd been dating for the past several months, standing on the front step of the church. Lori smiled. Coming here today had been the right move.

"Mrs. McCashlin?"

Lori turned to find the minister standing beside her, his hand extended.

"Actually I'm Lori Loveland, Molly and Nicole's nanny," she said, taking his hand.

"I'm sorry. I assumed Drew had remarried. I'm Pastor Steve Wilson. I wanted to welcome you." The minister's smile was warm and friendly. "We've missed the girls. And Drew. I hope he'll be joining you next week?"

"I'm not sure," Lori said with a noncommittal smile.

The minister's brow furrowed. "Does he still blame God for Karen's death?"

"I'd like to help you, Pastor," Lori said slowly, choosing her words carefully. "But I'm just the nanny. Mr. McCashlin doesn't share his personal feelings with me. All I can tell you is he's made it very clear he wants his girls in church."

"Thank God for that," Pastor Steve said. His gaze shifted to Molly. "It's hard to see her so quiet. Before the accident, she was quite the little chatterbox.''

''She was?'' Lori widened her gaze. She'd always assumed Molly had been more reserved, like Nicole.

''Oh, my, yes.'' Pastor Steve shook his head, a smile of remembrance on his lips. ''Molly never shut up. Karen used to laugh and swear Molly came out of the womb talking.''

Sadness washed over Lori at the thought of the blow life had dealt the little girl. ''Life isn't fair.''

''God never promised a life without pain or sorrow,'' the pastor said. ''But He did promise that He will carry our burdens.''

The minister patted Lori on the shoulder. ''I'm glad you brought her to church, Ms. Loveland. She needs God and her church family.''

Lori's gaze shifted from Molly to Nicole. She agreed. Everyone needed God in their life. She'd do her part and bring the girls to church every week.

But what would happen after she left? Who would bring them then?

And what about Drew? Who would bring *him?* Though he would deny it, he needed God's grace and strength as much as his daughters did.

If only he would realize that, until he reconciled with God, he'd never find true peace. Or happiness.

* * *

"Where are you and Susan going tonight?" Nicole plopped down on the sofa in the suite adjoining her father's bedroom. She still couldn't believe she'd been so foolish. At dinner when her father had announced he had a date, Nicole had assumed the worse. But thankfully she'd been wrong.

"We're going to check out the jazz festival." Drew looked at his reflection in the antique mirror on the wall. "Does this look too casual?"

Nicole narrowed her gaze and studied her father. Brown leather loafers. Khaki pants. Hunter-green polo. "You look fine."

"You really think so?"

Nicole frowned. Her father never asked for advice. He was the most self-confident, self-assured guy she knew. But tonight he was as nervous as a teenager going out on a first date. If she didn't know better, Nicole would think he wasn't going out with Susan at all, but rather with someone new. "You're going to a jazz concert, not a business meeting."

Drew cast one last look in the mirror. "I guess it'll do."

"You did say you're going out with Susan? Right?"

He nodded. "She's not a big jazz fan, but she's trying."

"You two have been going out for a while."

Nicole forced a casual tone. "Are things… serious?"

Drew shrugged. "I'm not sure if I'm ready to get serious with anyone. But if I ever did get to that point, would it bother you?"

Nicole hesitated. Though she abhorred the thought of a stepmother, she forced herself to look on the bright side. If her dad and Susan hooked up, it would guarantee Lori couldn't weasel her way into his affections.

"I want you to be happy, Dad," Nicole said smoothly, shooting him a phony smile. "And I'm sure you'd never be involved with a woman who didn't want Molly or me."

"Of course not," her father said immediately, looking shocked she'd even suggest otherwise. "You two come first. You know that."

Nicole heaved a sigh of relief. Maybe she'd worried all these days for nothing. Maybe the "torrid love affair" Lori spoke of hadn't been an affair at all. Maybe it had just been a one-night stand, a momentary insanity that had more to do with lust than love. Nicole could only hope he now realized getting involved with Lori had been a mistake, and that it would only make him appreciate Susan more.

"You and Susan have a good time," Nicole said. "Stay out as late as you want. I'll be home all night."

"Thanks again for baby-sitting Molly."

Nicole just smiled. She knew he appreciated it. And though he had this thing against paying family members for helping out, the fact that he wouldn't be seeing Lori tonight was payment enough.

Unless, of course, she could get him to take her to the mall this week. And maybe look at a couple of DVDs she'd been wanting....

The seats Susan had picked were located in the area closest to the stage. The view of the performers was great, but Drew's gaze couldn't help but wander to the grassy area farther back.

He took one last look. Though Lori hadn't said where she and Tom were going, Drew had the feeling they'd be at the festival. He'd even dressed with special care just in case their paths did cross.

"We should have brought a blanket," Drew murmured. "We could have sat back there and listened to the music for free."

"Please don't tell me you think mingling with the masses would be fun." Susan's gaze lingered on a group of older teens whose bare arms vividly showed the results of multiple trips to a tattoo artist. "Look who you'd be sitting with. It's the dregs of society back there."

Drew thought about drawing her attention to the young couple with a toddler, or the older gentleman and his grandson, but he knew he'd be wasting his breath.

Susan was an intelligent woman, but once she made up her mind, there was no changing it. He could understand, because he was like that, too.

So, instead of arguing the point, he changed the subject and they talked easily while the next musician set up. Drew was struck again by how many friends they had in common.

"I'm surprised our paths didn't cross years ago," Drew said. "We know so many of the same people."

"Actually," Susan said with a smile, "we did meet. Remember the big New Year's Eve party Rod and Gayle threw about five years ago?"

Drew's brows drew together and he thought for a moment. "Wasn't that another party where they had an ice sculpture?"

"That's the one," Susan said with a smile. "I'd come with a couple of friends and you were there with your wife."

A puzzled frown crossed Drew's face. "Were we introduced?"

"In a way." Susan laughed. "Don't you remember? I bumped into you and spilled champagne down the front of your jacket."

Drew lifted his shoulders in a slight shrug. The only things he remembered from that party were the elaborate ice sculpture...and his wife's dress.

Karen had never looked lovelier. Her low-cut black gown had fit like it had been designed with her in mind, flattering her slender figure and enhancing her softly rounded curves. His wife had been the object of many admiring glances that evening.

His heart twisted. Karen had been so vibrant, so alive. It was still hard to believe she was gone.

"You're doing it again." Though her smile was teasing, a hint of exasperation crept into Susan's tone.

Drew blinked. "What are you talking about?"

"I'm talking about the fact that your thoughts are elsewhere," Susan said. "You're paying absolutely no attention to me. Just like back then. The entire time we talked, your eyes were on your wife."

Drew stared. If he didn't know better, he'd think Susan had been jealous. But that was crazy. He'd been a married man whose primary focus had been on his wife, not on the single women in the room.

"I'll admit she did look lovely that evening," Susan continued. "I still remember her dress."

"Karen was a beautiful woman," Drew said. "Inside and out."

"How can any woman hope to take her place?" Susan asked softly.

No one will, Drew thought to himself. "I'm not looking for someone to take her place."

"I thought you told me once you eventually wanted to marry again."

"I do," Drew said. "But she won't take Karen's place. She'll have her own place in my life."

"And in your heart?" Susan asked in a low tone.

"Of course," Drew said quickly, even though he had doubts he'd ever find anyone as wonderful as Karen again.

Susan studied his face for a long moment.

"I've been offered a position with the San Francisco Arts council," she said finally. "It's a great opportunity."

Stunned, Drew sat back in his seat. He hadn't even known Susan was considering jobs out of state. "Are you going to take it?"

"It depends." Susan lowered her gaze and brushed a piece of lint from her sleeve. "Do you want me to stay?"

He hesitated, sensing she was asking for more than just career advice. Drew reached over and took her hand. "I want you to do whatever makes you happy."

"I'm turning forty next month." She lifted her gaze to meet his. "I'm too old to play games."

"I'm not playing games," Drew said. "I've always been honest with you."

"Okay. Let's talk honest." Susan straightened her shoulders and lifted her chin. "Tell me what

you think the odds are of us getting together...permanently.''

"You mean get married?'' Drew couldn't keep
the surprise from his voice.

"You sound shocked,'' Susan said. "Are you
telling me the thought never crossed your mind?''

Of course the thought had crossed his mind. After all, he and Susan had so much in common. All
his friends said she'd make him a perfect wife.

The problem was her kisses left him cold. At
first he'd wondered if his passion had died with
Karen. But then he'd met Lori, and realized the
fire still burned hot as ever.

Just not for Susan.

"I'm not ready to think about marriage,'' Drew
said softly, trying to be as gentle as possible. "I'm
not sure I'll ever be.''

The hope that had been stirring in Susan's eyes
faded. "That's too bad because I can tell you right
now that I want to get married. Maybe even have
a child. I can't afford to waste time dating someone
who isn't interested in commitment.''

He opened his mouth to say it wasn't that he
was against commitment, now just wasn't the right
time. But Drew shut his mouth without speaking.
He wouldn't hurt her anymore. And to give her
false hope would be wrong.

Because he knew that all the time in the world
wouldn't change one fact: Susan Tobin wasn't the
woman for him.

Chapter Nine

American Teen

Dear Lorelei Love,
I've always been a size ten, while most of
my friends are twos or fours. Last week one
of my girlfriends offered me some pills that
she said would help me lose weight. I'm not
really into putting chemicals into my body,
but I'd really like to wear a bikini before the
summer's over.

Fat in Fargo

Dear Fat,
Though it can be hard to hold out against
peer pressure, stand firm. Drugs can have a
lot of side effects, some you can't even imag-

ine. Go natural; increase your exercise, decrease your portion size and drink more water. I guarantee the weight will come off and you'll feel great in the process.

LL

Lori stopped in front of the open tent, her gaze lingering appreciatively on the paintings displayed inside.

"C'mon, Lori." Tom grabbed her hand. "We're heading over to the beer garden."

Swallowing her irritation, Lori smiled regretfully at the artist and followed Tom. When he'd asked her to go to the jazz festival she'd thought it was going to be the two of them. Instead they'd ended up going with a whole group of his friends.

Which was okay, because Lori was eager to meet people her own age. Unfortunately, everyone but she had attended Northwestern, and four out of the five were from the Chicago area. Though she tried to be friendly and participate in the conversations, most of the talk seemed to center around people she didn't know.

"Want another beer?" Tom asked as they moved into the line behind his friend.

Lori shook her head. She'd already had one, and by the way Tom was chugging them down, it looked as if she was destined to be the designated driver this evening. "I'll just have a soda."

"A soda?" Max, one of Tom's new roommates, made a gagging noise. He draped an arm companionably around her shoulders giving her a squeeze and a wink. "It's Saturday night. Time to loosen up. Enjoy life."

Lori slipped out of Max's grasp. If there was anything she hated it was an obnoxious drunk.

"Lay off her, Max." Tom shot Lori a supportive smile. "Lori's a working girl. She can't afford to get wasted tonight."

"Work?" Tiffany, Max's date for the evening, raised a brow. "I thought you wrote a magazine column."

"I do," Lori said. "But I'm also a nanny."

"A nanny." Sarah, the other woman in the group, stared as if Lori had suddenly grown horns. "Why in the world would you ever do that?"

"I need the money," Lori said simply, refusing to make excuses. "And I like children."

"Really?" Sarah and Tiffany exchanged glances.

Lori groaned to herself. She wished Tom hadn't brought up her job. It hadn't taken her long to figure out that this group had no idea what it meant to live on a budget. Though she didn't begrudge them the good fortune of being born wealthy, she didn't want them to pity her for her more modest beginnings.

"Who do you nanny for?" Tiffany raised a perfectly arched brow and Lori had the impression she was asking more out of politeness than any real interest.

"Clay McCashlin's younger sisters," Tom said before Lori could answer. "You remember Clay?"

Tom's friends nodded.

"Lori and Clay are *good* friends," Tom said in a tone Lori guessed was anything but casual.

Suddenly she was part of the group again. But even as Lori plastered a bright smile on her face, she found herself glancing at her watch and wondering when the evening would be over.

She wasn't sorry when the others decided they'd had enough jazz and cut out early, leaving her and Tom to wander over to the concert area alone.

They found a spot under a large shade tree and took a seat on the ground. She leaned against Tom's shoulder and listened to the music, trying to push the thoughts of Drew from her mind.

"You haven't been yourself this evening." Tom pulled his attention from the stage and his gaze lingered on her face. "Is something the matter?"

"Not at all," Lori said. "I'm having a great time."

"You sure?" Tom's gaze turned sharp and assessing. "You seem stressed to me."

Lori lifted one shoulder in a casual shrug. "Maybe I am. I've had a lot going on lately."

"I've got just what you need." Tom glanced

around, then pulled a thin cigarette from his pocket. "A few puffs of this and you'll be feelin' fine."

Lori widened her eyes. Though they sat with their backs to a tree and darkness surrounded them, there were people less than ten feet away.

"Put that away," she whispered furiously. "Someone's going to see."

To her horror, Tom laughed and pulled out a lighter. "You worry like an old lady."

Her hand snapped the lighter shut. "I mean it, Tom!"

Tom stared at her for a long moment, then put the lighter and the joint back in his pocket.

"It's just weed," he said at last.

"I don't do drugs," Lori said, the words sounding stilted even to her ears. Unfortunately, she didn't know another way to make her feelings clear. "Of any kind."

"You know, when I first met you I thought you were cool." He shook his head. "But I'm finding out you really are just a small-town girl."

Lori lifted her chin. "I'll take that as a compliment."

The evening went downhill from there, although Tom had mellowed somewhat by the time she dropped him off.

But when he tried to pull her into his arms, Lori stepped back. Their relationship was over. Tom had a lot of good qualities, but he wasn't the man for her. What had happened tonight had shown her that.

Back at home, Lori stood on the porch for a long time staring up at the stars.

Dear God, all my life I've put my own needs last. Now it's my turn. I want to have fun, but I also want someone to love. Unfortunately I'm not doing so well finding him on my own. Please lead me to that special guy. I'm putting myself in Your hands. Amen.

Lori had barely finished her prayer when she heard the front door open. She turned and found herself face-to-face with Drew McCashlin.

"I thought I heard someone out here." Drew opened the door wide. His gaze slid to her sleeveless sundress. "Come on in."

"Don't mind if I do," Lori said lightly, flashing him a smile. "It's getting chilly out here."

"I know," Drew said, pulling the door closed as she brushed past him. "I was at the jazz festival tonight, and by the time we left, I found myself wishing I'd brought a jacket."

"You were there?" Lori stopped suddenly. "I was there, too."

"Susan and I were sitting close to the stage," he said. "Where were you?"

"Toward the back." Lori waved a vague hand.

"Tom and I sat in the grass. He thought it would be more fun."

"And was it?"

"It was okay," she said with a shrug. "How was your evening?"

"Okay," Drew said. "Susan and I decided not to see each other anymore."

"Why?" The word popped out before Lori could remind herself that the reason was none of her business.

A look of discomfort crossed Drew's face. "Our relationship wasn't going anywhere."

Though the statement was vague, Lori understood immediately. "She wanted a commitment. You didn't."

Drew shrugged, not confirming her suspicions, but not denying them, either. "How about you and Tom? Are you two still together?"

Lori rested her hand on the post at the bottom of the stairs. She forced the same casual tone he'd used with her only moments before. "I don't think we'll be seeing each other anymore."

"Really?" Drew lifted a brow. "Want to talk about it?"

"Do you want to talk about you and Susan?"

Drew smiled. "Touché."

"I could use a drink," Lori said. "What about you?"

"Hot cocoa?"

"What else?"

Drew's smile widened. "Lead the way."

A half hour later, Lori sat with Drew in the kitchen licking the last sticky bit of marshmallow from her spoon. She lifted her gaze to find Drew's focus on her lips.

A shiver of awareness traveled up Lori's spine.

His eyes darkened.

Lori stood quickly and gathered up the empty cups. "I'll just put these in the sink."

But as she rounded the table, Drew's hand reached out and grabbed her arm. "Mrs. Graham can do that."

"I don't mind," Lori said. "I'm used to cleaning up after myself."

His gaze met hers. "You're a remarkable woman."

Lori's cheeks warmed.

"When I was with Susan this evening, I found myself wishing it were you beside me," he said softly.

Though his words sent a flood of heat flowing though her veins, Lori forced a light tone. "Only because you feel safe with me. You know I'm not out to get married."

Drew chuckled. "At least not to an old guy with kids."

"True," Lori said. "But for an old guy you can be lots of fun. And I have to admit, when I was with Tom, I found myself wishing I was with you, too."

"Which goes to prove we're still on the same wavelength." Drew stood, took the cups from her hands and placed them back on the table. "Why didn't we go together?"

"You didn't ask," Lori said softly.

He moved closer and tilted her face up with his finger. "I'm asking now. Will you go out with me Friday night?"

"I can't," Lori said. His closeness made her voice husky. "You forget. I'm a nanny and I'm scheduled to work next Friday."

"I know your boss pretty well." Drew gently brushed back a strand of her hair with his hand. "I think I can get you some time off."

Lori reached up and encircled his neck with her arms. "You'd do that for me?"

"No problem," he said, lowering his mouth to hers.

Nicole shut the door to her sister's room and moved to the top of the stairs. While reading to Molly, she'd sworn she'd heard voices downstairs.

But how could that be? Her dad had come home hours ago from his date with Susan and Mrs. Graham had the night off.

She crept down the stairs and followed the voices to the kitchen. The door was closed and

Nicole paused, strangely reluctant to intrude. Laughter sounded on the other side of the door and Nicole's heart leapt to her throat when she heard Lori's voice mingled with her father's baritone.

Nicole's hands tightened into fists at her side. The nanny was a predator, pure and simple. She'd set her sights on her rich employer and she wasn't going to stop until she had him.

Anger rose inside Nicole and, without a hint of warning, she flung the door open.

Her father and Lori sprang apart.

Nicole's gaze pinned her father. His hair, disheveled, looked like someone had been running their fingers through it, and she could see traces of lipstick on his neck.

"Nicole." Her father spoke first. "What are you still doing up?"

She lifted her chin and breezed past him. "I was thirsty. I wanted a drink. You have a problem with that?"

"Of course not," Drew said, his jaw tightening at her curt tone.

Taking a glass from the cupboard, Nicole turned just in time to see her father and Lori exchange a glance.

"Did I interrupt something?" Nicole asked.

Lori shook her head and smiled. "Your father and I both went to the jazz festival tonight. We were just comparing notes."

Nicole lifted a brow. "Is that what it's called?"

"Nicole!" The word shot from Drew's lips.

Nicole could tell her father was angry but she was past caring. If she didn't stop this relationship, her worst fears would be realized.

The problem was she didn't have a clue what to do next.

Chapter Ten

American Teen

Dear Lorelei Love,
My problem is my mother. Since she and my dad divorced last year, she's lost twenty pounds and dyed her hair blond. She's even started wearing some of my clothes. My friends laugh and say it's like something out of a TV sitcom, but I don't think it's so funny.

Now she's started dating and some of these guys look like they're barely out of college. She's out of control. What can I do?

Sleepless in Sausalito

Dear Sleepless,
Divorce can be very traumatic and it appears it dealt quite a blow to your mother's self-

esteem. What she needs is understanding. But while you're being understanding, tell her you're not into sharing clothes. Then offer to take her shopping. You should be able to help her find her something trendy that doesn't look like it came from the junior department. Next step is to find her a hairdresser who can highlight her hair without making her look like she should be walking down by the pier picking up sailors.

In terms of the men she dates, try to look at each one as individuals and don't badmouth them. Otherwise she may be tempted to hold on to one that she should cut loose.

LL

"Are you sure you don't want to go to Navy Pier with us?" Keys in hand, Lori paused at the kitchen door, Molly at her side.

Lori knew it had upset Nicole to see her with Drew last Saturday night. But it was Wednesday now and the girl had barely said five words to her.

Nicole leaned back in her chair and stared at Lori. "How many times do I have to tell you? I'm having lunch with my grandmother today."

Lori's fingers tightened around the keys. This was the first time Nicole had mentioned having plans. When Lori had asked earlier, the teen had only said she didn't "feel" like going.

Nicole's condescending tone seemed designed to goad a response. But Lori had been through this many times with her brothers and sisters and she knew if she reacted, she'd be playing right into Nicole's hand.

"That should be fun for you," Lori said lightly, then shifted her gaze to Molly. "I guess it'll be just you and I, kiddo."

"Good. I caught you before you left." A familiar masculine voice sounded behind Lori.

Lori whirled, her lips curving upward in a welcoming smile. "Drew."

She hadn't seen him all week. He'd been closing an important business deal and he'd been up and out of the house every morning before she and the girls even sat down for breakfast. And every evening he'd arrived home long after they'd all gone to bed.

"Hello, ladies." Drew planted a kiss on the top of Molly's head and smiled at Lori.

"You closed the deal, didn't you?" The instant Lori had seen his face she'd known the news was good.

"Sure did." He grinned. "We got everything we wanted and then some."

"Excuse me. I need to get ready." Nicole pushed back her chair with a clatter and stood.

Drew widened his gaze. "Nicole. I didn't see you back there."

"I know," Nicole said. "You were too busy looking elsewhere." The teen's gaze shifted pointedly to Lori.

Drew's expression stilled. His gaze flickered briefly over Lori before and turned back to Nicole.

"Well, anyway I'm glad you're here," he said. "And don't worry about changing. You look fine. After all, we're just going to the Pier."

"We're?" Nicole had reached the doorway, but she stopped suddenly and turned to face him. "*You're* coming?"

Drew nodded and Lori could sense his confusion at her unexpected response.

"I haven't been around much this past week," he said. "I thought this would be a good chance for us to spend some time together. Maybe eat at that little place you like so much...."

"Why didn't you let me know earlier?" The glinting glance Nicole shot Lori made it clear that the girl thought Lori had something to do with her father's sudden change in plans.

"I'm sorry, honey," Drew said. "But I wasn't sure when I'd get those final papers signed. I didn't want to say I'd come and then have to disappoint you girls by canceling at the last minute."

"Well, it's too late now. I've already made plans

with Gram,'' Nicole said. ''We'll have to reschedule the trip to Navy Pier for another time.''

Molly's head jerked up and a noise of protest slipped past her lips.

Drew's gaze shot to the little girl. ''Molly?''

Lori's breath caught in her throat.

Molly lowered her gaze and moved closer to Lori. Lori crossed her fingers that Drew wouldn't cancel their trip to the Pier. Though Molly had made such sounds before, it was definitely an encouraging sign. If Drew wanted to reinforce Molly's response, there was no better way to do that than to go forward with their original plans.

Drew shifted his attention back to his oldest daughter. ''Last week you told me you were excited about spending the day at the Pier.''

Nicole pulled her gaze from her sister. ''I changed my mind. Grandma and I talked and I decided to go to lunch with her instead.''

''I'm sorry to hear that.'' Drew shook his head and regret filled his eyes. ''But I can't deprive Molly of the outing she's been counting on just because you chose to make other plans.''

A smile touched Molly's lips and Lori could feel the little girl relax.

''You just want to spend time with *her*.'' Nicole cast Lori a venomous glance. ''It doesn't have anything to do with not wanting to disappoint Molly.''

"Nicole Marie." Drew's lips tightened and his eyes flashed. "That's enough."

"I'm going to my room." Nicole lifted her chin and met his censuring gaze head-on. "Have Mrs. Graham call me when Gram gets here."

Nicole flounced out of the room, not even bothering to say goodbye to her sister.

"Teenagers." Drew muttered the word like a curse. "She certainly is in a mood today."

"You know how it is when you're that age," Lori said with a shrug. "Everything is a big deal."

"Maybe so." Drew's gaze shifted to Molly. "But I'm not going to worry about it right now. I've got more important things on my mind."

"Such as?" Lori lifted a brow.

"Such as," Drew said with a smile, "figuring out how I'm going to convince both of you beautiful ladies to go on the Ferris wheel with me."

The little café in Highland Park was one of Nicole's favorites, but today the food might as well have been sawdust. Though she was barely halfway through her club sandwich, Nicole couldn't force herself to eat another bite.

She shoved the plate aside and heaved a heavy sigh, a sudden tightness gripping her chest.

"What's the matter, honey?" Celia reached across the table and took her granddaughter's hand. "You haven't been yourself all day. And don't tell me nothing is wrong because I know better. First you couldn't find anything you liked at Anthropologie and now you've barely touched your lunch.''

"It's nothing, Gram." Nicole blinked back tears at her grandmother's concern. "You wouldn't understand anyway."

"You just try me," Celia said. "I understand more than you know."

Nicole shook her head. Her grandmother was a wonderful woman but she'd always been a staunch supporter of her son-in-law.

"It's about your father and the nanny, isn't it?" Her grandmother sat back in her chair and gazed thoughtfully at Nicole. "You're worried about the two of them 'hooking up.'"

The words sounded so strange coming from her grandmother that Nicole had to smile. But the unpleasant reality of the situation pulled the smile from her lips.

"According to her, they've already 'hooked up,'" Nicole said, unable to keep the bitterness from her tone as she remembered Lori's boastful words in that coffee shop. "They've already had sex."

"What?" Celia Barrett dropped her cup into its china saucer with a clatter. "She told you that she and your father—"

"—were having a torrid love affair," Nicole interrupted, finishing her grandmother's sentence. "Actually, she didn't tell me. She was bragging about it to someone else and I overheard. And the 'torrid love affair' bit are her words, not mine."

"I can't say that I'm surprised your father is starting to date again." The older woman signaled the waiter for the check.

Nicole stared, amazed her grandmother could be so calm. She didn't even seem upset that her son-in-law was having an affair with his children's nanny.

"The problem is they aren't just dating. They're—"

"I know, my dear." Celia raised her hand, stopping Nicole from repeating her story. "Let me continue. Though I'm not surprised your father is dating, I *would* be surprised to find out he's involved in a physical relationship, be—"

"But Lori said—"

"Nicole." Her grandmother's tone was firm. "What have I told you about interrupting your elders?"

"Sorry, Gram." Nicole lowered her gaze, her hands twisting the napkin in her lap. She should have known better than to think her grandmother would be on her side.

"Honey, look at me." Though her grandmother's tone might be no-nonsense, the older woman's eyes were filled with understanding. "I understand how concerned you are, but I have to tell you the Drew McCashlin I know would never engage in a meaningless affair with one of his employees. He may not attend church anymore but he's always held himself and others to a strict moral code. I can't see any reason he'd abandon those beliefs now.''

Nicole waited a minute before speaking, wanting to be absolutely sure her grandmother had finished.

''I can think of several reasons. It's been two years since Mom died,'' Nicole said. A tiny stab of pain knifed her heart at the thought of her mother. ''He's turned his back on God. Maybe he no longer cares what the Bible says about sex outside of marriage.''

''Nicole, I—''

This time it was Nicole who raised a hand, stopping the interruption. ''He's forty-three years old, Gram. And she's young, beautiful and convenient.''

''You really believe that's what is happening?''

Nicole hesitated then nodded.

''I can't believe it.'' Nicole's grandmother shook her head, her voice filled with dismay. ''Are you sure you didn't misunderstand?''

Nicole shook her head. She almost wished there had been some mistake. But she knew what she'd heard. ''What are we going to do?''

''You, my dear, are going to do nothing except

continue to be a sweet, loving girl.'' Celia patted her hand.

Sweet, loving girl? Nicole groaned. Could this day get any worse?

"If I'm going to do nothing," Nicole said slowly, eyeing her grandmother with undisguised suspicion, "what are you going to do?"

"Why, my dear, I'm surprised you need to ask." Her grandmother favored her with a bright smile. "I'm going to talk with your father and get us some answers."

Chapter Eleven

American Teen

Dear Lorelei Love,
I've been in gymnastics since I could walk. But now that I'm in high school I'm tired of it. My parents can't believe I want to quit the team. They've tried everything to convince me that I'm making a big mistake. But I don't think I am. Whose life is it anyway?

Irritated in Indianapolis

Dear Irritated,
Parents often think they have all the answers, but you're right, this is your life and your decision. Maybe it would help if you made a list of why you want to quit the team and

discussed it with them. That way they could see that this isn't an impulsive decision but rather a well thought out plan.

LL

Lori decided that though the day had gotten off to a rocky start, it was definitely looking up. The drive to Navy Pier had gone smoothly despite the heavy traffic, and just as they were pulling into a nearby parking lot, someone in the front row pulled out, freeing a space for Drew's truck.

Lori had brought sweaters along for her and Molly, but tossed them back on the seat after stepping outside and feeling the warmth on her bare arms.

"It's going to be hot today." Lori heaved a happy sigh and lifted her face to the bright sun.

Drew smiled and Lori had to smile back.

"You look nice and cool." Drew's gaze lingered on her cotton skirt and matching shirt. "Like orange sherbet."

A shiver of pleasure traveled up her spine. "They call this shade orange parfait."

Drew's smile widened. "Sherbet or parfait, all I know is you look delectable."

Molly pulled on her father's hand, seemingly impatient.

The sudden warmth in Lori's cheeks had little to do with the heat of the sun. Instead of remembering who she was and why she was here, she was acting like some love-struck schoolgirl on a date.

Lori looked down at the little girl. "I think I'd like to ride on the Ferris wheel first. How about you?"

Molly nodded, her eyes sparkling.

"The Ferris wheel it is." Drew placed his hand on his daughter's shoulder. "After all, this is your day. I want you to have a good time."

Molly grinned and she skipped happily between them, holding tight to her father's hand. Drew cast a sideways glance at Lori. "I'm glad you came with us."

"I am, too," Lori said, reveling in the feel of the sun on her shoulders, the smell of fried onions wafting on the breeze and the bustle of the crowd. "Although I hope I'm not intruding on your father-daughter time."

"You're a nice addition to our father-daughter time," Drew said gallantly. "What do you say, Molly? Are you glad Lori came with us today?"

Molly stopped and turned unexpectedly. She reached out and slipped her hand into Lori's and smiled.

"I'd say that's your answer," Drew said, his smile widening.

Though there were many specialty restaurants in the area, when it came time to pick where they'd eat, Molly didn't hesitate. She grabbed their hands and pulled them into McDonald's. Drew glanced at Lori over the top of Molly's head, apology in his eyes.

Lori flashed him a smile before turning her attention to Molly.

"I'm glad we're going to eat here." Lori lifted her gaze to the menu board. "I've been dying for a Big Mac."

Drew looked at her in surprise. "You're going to order a Big Mac?"

Lori nodded. "And some fries and a shake. But don't worry, I've got money."

"It's not about the money." Drew chuckled. His gaze surveyed Lori's figure. "Susan would never think of eating a Big Mac. Or fries. With her it was always a salad. With fat-free dressing."

Lori wrinkled her nose. "Bor-ing."

To Drew's surprise, Molly wrinkled her nose, imitating Lori.

"Okay." Drew laughed. "No salad today."

By the time they'd reached the front of the line Drew decided to go all out and get a Big Mac, too. Molly got a Happy Meal, with pickles only, just the way she liked it.

"It looks like there's a table over by the window," Lori said. "How about Molly and I go grab it?"

"Good idea." Drew handed the teenager behind the counter several bills. "I'll pick up the straws and ketchup and meet you there."

Lori rested her hand on Molly's shoulder as they wove their way through the crowded restaurant. Drew's heart twisted. How many times had he watched Karen do the very same thing?

He shoved the memory aside, not wanting even a hint of sadness to taint the outing. So far it had been a great day. Not only had Molly almost talked, but there had been several times today she'd been like her old self, her blue eyes dancing with pleasure, her lips turned up in a wide smile.

The only thing missing was her endless chatter, but after today he had renewed hope that it would come.

Though none of them had complained about being particularly hungry, they attacked the food like lumberjacks who'd been working all day.

Lori leaned back with a contented sign. "That was every bit as good as I remembered."

Drew glanced down at his almost full carton of fries and then at her tray. Not only had she eaten her Big Mac and all her fries, but she'd finished off her shake, as well. "How can you eat so much and stay so thin?"

"I have a pretty good metabolism," Lori said, wiping her mouth with the corner of a napkin. "Plus I don't eat like this all the time."

Lori smiled at Molly. "And how is your lunch, Miss Molly?"

Though the conversation-shift to Molly seemed effortless, Drew recognized the concerted effort Lori was making, and had in fact been making all morning, to draw Molly out, to make her feel a part of the conversation.

His heart warmed at Lori's thoughtfulness. It had been his experience that most adults tended to ignore his youngest daughter. Since she'd quit talking, Molly had tended to blend into the woodwork. And her unexplained silence seemed to make people uncomfortable. Regardless, when they hurt her with their disinterest, they hurt him, as well.

But when Molly smiled broadly in response to Lori's attention, he couldn't help but smile, too.

"Anyone up for some dessert?" Lori's eyes sparkled.

Molly sat straight in her seat and nodded eagerly.

"Dessert?" Drew groaned. "After all we just ate?"

Lori laughed. "I'm thinking of something light and fluffy, something that will just melt in our mouths."

It took Drew only an instant to realize the direction of her thoughts. He'd seen her gaze linger on the stand located near the Ferris wheel. "Cotton candy."

"Exactly." Lori grinned. She looked at Molly. "Rainbow-colored. Did you see it?"

Molly nodded and looked at her father. He could see the question in her eyes.

"Okay," he said with an exaggerated sigh. "But I don't want you two blaming me if your stomachs get upset."

Lori's lip twitched and he could tell she was trying hard not to laugh.

Drew groaned. "You know who I sound like, don't you?"

"My mother?" Lori asked, the twinkle in her eye even more pronounced.

"No," he said. "Mine."

They all laughed, and for just a second, Lori felt part of the family.

"I love this stuff." Lori stuck another wad of the spun sugar into her mouth.

"I couldn't tell," Drew said teasingly. He still couldn't believe she could pack that much food away in that flat stomach.

"Molly likes it, too," Lori said, smiling down at the little girl.

"Mmm-hmm," Molly said, licking the last of the sticky sweetness from her lips.

Drew stilled at the unfamiliar sound. Though Molly had laughed and cried over the past two years, she'd never verbalized anything more. Now, twice in one day...

"Thank you, God." Drew couldn't stop from sending a prayer heavenward. It felt both awkward and familiar to pray to the God he'd ignored for the past two years. But how could he not say thanks when his heart overflowed with happiness?

"What do you two want to do next?" Drew asked. "I thought we—"

"Drew McCashlin, I didn't expect to see you here."

Drew turned to the sound of the familiar voice.

"I could say the same thing." A welcoming smile lifted Drew's lips. "I didn't know you'd taken the day off."

Gary Miller was a senior accountant at McCashlin Enterprises. He and his wife, Ann, had once been frequent visitors at Drew's home.

"Ann's sister and her family are in town from Nebraska." Gary gestured to a group waiting in line at the Ferris wheel.

Drew waved, even though the only two he recognized were Gary's dark-haired wife and little girl, Amy.

He quickly introduced Lori, then shifted his attention back to Gary's family.

"Amy sure has gotten big," Drew said. "She must have grown three or four inches."

"It's been a while since you've seen her," Gary said. "Almost two years."

Ever since Karen died.

Though neither of them voiced the thought, the words hung unspoken in the air between them.

"I was glad to see the girls in church Sunday," Gary said finally, filling the silence. "And Amy was thrilled. She's really missed Molly."

Drew's gaze shot to Lori.

Lori just smiled and took another bite of cotton candy. Her gaze dropped to Molly who stood next to her waving at Amy.

"Would you mind if Molly went on the Ferris wheel with Amy?" Gary asked. "Amy's cousins are all boys, and I hate to say it but she hasn't been having that much fun today."

Drew lowered his gaze to his daughter. "Do you want to go with Amy?"

To his surprise, Molly slanted a sideways glance at Lori.

"Go ahead," Lori urged. "Your dad and I will be right over here waiting."

Seemingly satisfied, the little girl headed toward her friend without so much as a backward glance.

"Thanks, Gary," Drew said.

"No thanks necessary," Gary said. "We're your friends. We've missed seeing you and your girls."

Drew's gaze drifted to a point over Gary's left shoulder. He knew he'd hurt Gary and Ann by rejecting their repeated offers of friendship these past two years, but every time he saw the happy couple it reminded him of what he'd lost. "It's been a rough couple of years."

"I know it has." Gary clapped him on the shoulder. "But always remember, we're here for you. And God is there for you, too. Will we see you in church on Sunday?"

"He'll be there," Lori said unexpectedly.

Drew didn't have any choice but to play along. But the minute Gary returned to his family, Drew turned to Lori and narrowed his gaze. "What was that about?"

Lori flashed him a bright smile. "Let's talk in the shade. If I don't get out of this sun, I'm going to look like a lobster tomorrow."

Without waiting for his response she turned and headed toward a bench under a nearby tree. As he followed, Drew couldn't help but notice how she was garnering admiring glances from a group of men standing nearby.

Drew squared his shoulders. He'd never let a woman—no matter how attractive she was—tell him what he was going to do. And he wasn't about to start now.

Lori's heart pounded in her chest. Whatever had made her say that to Gary? She knew how Drew felt about attending church, especially *that* church. And it certainly wasn't her place to answer for him.

She walked slowly, using the time to not only figure out why she'd done it, but what she was going to say in her own defense.

The problem was, she didn't feel like apologizing. She still believed he needed to be in church with his girls.

Dear God. I've never been one to ask for much, but Drew needs You. Help me say the right words, words that will make him realize what he's been missing. Amen.

Lori took a seat on the bench and crossed one leg over the other, waiting for Drew to sit down. But he remained standing.

She swallowed hard and lifted her chin.

"We need to get one thing clear," he said in a firm tone that brooked no argument. "No one speaks for me. If I want to go to church, I will. If I don't want to go, I won't. But I don't need you making those decisions for me."

"I understand," Lori said. "I just thought—"

"You thought what?"

"That you have a lot to be thankful for." Lori cast a pointed glance in the direction to where Molly stood surrounded by the Miller family. She shifted her gaze back to Drew. "Can't you spare one morning a week to say thanks?"

Lori knew if Pastor Steve were in her place he'd

probably be quoting scriptures and talking about God's goodness and mercy. But Pastor Steve wasn't here and Lori had never had a good memory for Bible verses. So she was forced to resort to the method that had always worked with her brothers and sisters—guilt.

And she didn't feel one bit bad using it in this situation. Because deep inside she had the feeling getting Drew *inside* a church again would be a much-needed first step.

Drew's brows furrowed in thought. His gaze shifted, lingering on Molly as she climbed into the Ferris wheel car. In the bright sunshine her hair glistened like spun gold and, sandwiched in the seat between Amy and her mother, she looked like any other happy healthy seven-year-old.

With a sigh, Drew plopped down on the seat next to Lori. "You're right. Going to church one week isn't going to kill me."

"Who knows," Lori said in a deliberately light tone, "you may even like it."

"Lori," Drew growled, but any anger had long since left his eyes.

Lori laughed. Impulsively she lifted her hand to his face, touching his cheek with her fingers. "Has anyone ever told you how incredibly sexy you are when you growl?"

Surprise flickered across Drew's face, followed swiftly by desire. He captured her hand and pressed a kiss against her palm. The mere touch of his lips sent a shiver of excitement racing up her spine.

"Did anyone ever tell you how incredibly sexy you look when you smile?" he asked, his gaze never leaving hers.

Her heart picked up speed and her breath came in short puffs. "I smile all the time."

"I know," he said in a low growl.

Lori leaned closer. "You'd better be careful, I might have to smile some more."

"And then I might just have to do this...."

Drew's strong hand tilted her face to his and suddenly they were nose to nose, or—more importantly—mouth to mouth. His lips were only a heartbeat away from hers. He lowered his head and covered her mouth with his.

Lori looped her arms around his neck and he kissed her again and again, long, slow, lazy kisses that made her forget everything except him.

"I hate to interrupt..."

Lori's head jerked up at the masculine voice. She opened her eyes and blinked in the bright sunshine. Heat rose up her neck at the sight of Gary's amused smile. Her hands dropped to her side. She resisted the urge to smooth her hair.

Drew lifted his head and met Gary's gaze. "Is the ride over already?"

"They're just getting off now," Gary said.

"Ann and I were talking and we wondered if Molly could spend the night. Like I said earlier, Amy's the odd one out with all the boys."

"I'd be glad to bring her home in the morning." Ann walked up beside her husband, the two girls at her side. Her gaze shifted to linger fondly on Molly. "And don't worry about clothes or toothbrushes. The girls are about the same size so Molly can borrow pajamas and we've got extra toothbrushes at home. We'll take good care of her."

"Do you want to spend the night at Amy's house?" Drew asked.

Molly glanced at Amy and nodded eagerly.

Drew smiled. "Okay by me."

The girls jumped up and down. Ann laughed. "I'll have her home around ten in the morning."

"I'll be waiting," Lori said with a smile, giving Molly a quick hug.

Drew opened his arms to his daughter. "Don't I get one, too?"

Molly wrapped her arms around his neck and buried her head against his shoulder.

"You have a good time, honey." He planted a kiss against her hair.

"I love you, Daddy." The words were no more than a fleeting whisper on the wind. For a moment Drew thought she'd actually spoke. Until he realized that it had been only his own wishful thinking that had conjured up the once-familiar words.

"I almost said no," Drew said when Molly was out of earshot. "I know it sounds selfish but I really wanted to spend the rest of the day with her."

"Not selfish at all." An understanding look blanketed Lori's face. "You love your daughter. And that's why you said she could spend the night with Amy."

"She *was* excited." Drew shook his head. "You know when I hugged her, for a moment I swore she spoke. But I think I'm so anxious for her to talk I'm hearing words that aren't there."

"I bet it won't be long before she speaks," Lori said.

"What makes you think that?"

"Because she's started to verbalize," Lori said. Though her words were matter-of-fact, Drew could hear the underlying excitement in her tone. "That's a good beginning. You said the psychiatrist thought her lack of speech was tied to the trauma of the accident. It's been already two years. Maybe Molly is finally able to move forward."

Drew thought of how his daughter had been before the accident: a lively chatterbox that could talk anyone's ear off. Having her silent these past two years had been unbelievably hard. "I swear I'd go to church every week for the rest of my life if Molly would just start talking again."

"You know as well as I do," Lori pointed out gently, "that's not the way it works."

"You're right." Drew's lips tightened, remembering how he'd prayed that God would spare Karen. He hadn't listened then. Why should he expect God to listen now?

"Have you ever heard that God helps those who help themselves?" Lori asked.

Drew laughed. "I don't think I'm familiar with that particular Bible passage."

"Okay, so maybe it's not a specific verse, but you know what I mean."

Drew's gaze drifted to her lips and he couldn't help but notice they were still swollen from his kisses.

"I'm just saying that maybe Molly's improvement has been hastened by the fact that you're spending so much more time together."

"You might be on to something." Drew pondered Lori's words. "Every psychiatrist and psychologist that Molly ever saw said they felt she would one day talk again. And that the more secure and loved she felt, the better."

"That's why I think your decision to attend church on Sunday was a good one."

"Decision?" Drew snorted. "I was practically roped into it."

"Does that matter?" Lori raised a brow. "Roped into it or not, it's a wise move."

Drew gaze narrowed and he stared thoughtfully

at Lori. He wasn't stupid. He was on to her game. She was manipulating him.

But the funny thing was that fact didn't bother him in the least. Because he knew she had only Molly's good in mind.

And for that, he could forgive her almost anything.

Chapter Twelve

American Teen

Dear Lorelei Love,
My parents divorced when I was little, and I live with my dad. Everything was going fine until Dad's neighbor—also divorced—decided to go after him. She's half his age and pretty (if you like the Angelina Jolie look). Things are heating up between them and I'm afraid he's going to do something crazy.

Help!

Anxious in Albuquerque

Dear Anxious,
Other than her age, is there something else that makes you feel she wouldn't be a good

partner for your dad? If you do have concerns, I'd suggest talking to him. If he blows
you off, find someone whom he respects to
talk to him about "their" concerns. Good
luck!

LL

"How long is this going to take?" Nicole
plopped down on her grandmother's sofa, her gaze
shifting to the mantel clock. It was already eight
o'clock and Gram seemed in no hurry to take her
home. Nicole didn't want her father and Lori alone
together any longer than necessary. Molly was supposed to be with them but Nicole knew how
sneaky Lori could be. She'd probably already
found a way to ditch the little girl.

Nicole's lips tightened. Lori may be smart, but
Nicole was on to her games. And now that Gram
knew the score...

"What did you say, sweetheart?" Gram smiled
at Nicole and took a leisurely sip of tea.

"I asked how long this conference-call thing is
going to take." Nicole tried hard not to let her
irritation show. After all, Gram had made every
effort to show her a good time today and Nicole
appreciated it. But she had to get home, and the
sooner the better.

"They usually don't go longer than an hour."

Gram set her cup down and glanced at the thin watch encircling her wrist. ''And they should be calling any minute.''

''But what am I going to do all that time?'' Nicole hinted, hoping her grandmother would offer to have one of her staff drive her home.

Gram laughed. ''Oh, my dear. You're a smart girl. I'm sure you can figure out something.''

''But—''

''It will go fast,'' Gram said. ''I've got some new magazines or you can use the computer. The technicians were out yesterday and it now has its own line.''

''That's great, Gram. But the computer wasn't the reason I asked. I—''

''Mrs. Barrett.'' The maid appeared in the doorway. ''I'm sorry to interrupt, but Mrs. Jensen is on the phone.''

''Oops, sweetie, the Garden Club beckons.'' Flashing a brilliant smile, her grandmother hurried away, leaving Nicole alone.

Garden Club. An hour conference call to talk about some stupid fall festival? Nicole snorted. She certainly hoped she had better things to do with her time when she was her grandmother's age.

She should have known better. She should have insisted her grandmother take her home after they'd finished shopping in Highland Park. She should have…

Nicole shoved the recriminations aside. She'd agreed to the side trip to Long Grove. But she hadn't realized that her grandmother planned to comb every antique store for some special vase to add to her already-extensive collection.

By the time they'd finished shopping it had been almost six and her stomach was growling. If her grandmother hadn't suggested the Cheesecake Factory, hungry or not, Nicole would have passed on the dinner invitation.

After dinner, just when Nicole finally thought they were headed home, her grandmother had remembered the conference call and turned the Cadillac toward her house instead.

Nicole grabbed a magazine from the side table. "I'll be lucky to be home by ten."

A knot formed in the pit of Nicole's stomach but she told herself she didn't know *for sure* her dad and Lori were still together. For all she knew Lori could have had a date with Tom.

Nicole held the thought with a desperate hope. There was no use worrying about what was going on. She couldn't do anything until Gram got off the phone.

Heaving a resigned sigh, Nicole's gaze dropped to the magazine in her lap. Her eyes widened in surprise.

American Teen?

Nicole's appreciative gaze lingered on the

glossy cover. Not only was *A.T.* her favorite magazine, this was the current issue.

Last time when she'd been over she'd complained about the lack of decent magazines to read.
Gram had said she'd remedy the situation but Nicole had never dreamed she'd order *A.T.*

Nicole opened the magazine and eagerly
scanned the list of articles. It was hard to decide
which one to read first. Though she was tempted
to take the quiz on ''Are you and your guy com-
patible?'' she couldn't resist the advice column.

''Ask Lorelei Love'' had only been running as
a regular feature for the past couple of months, but
it already had a devoted following among Nicole's
friends.

Nicole read through the first two questions
quickly but when she got to the third one, her
breath caught in her throat. Though there were dif-
ferences in the situation—Lori was in no way as
hot as Angelina Jolie—in many ways the question
posed by Anxious in Albuquerque could have
come from her.

She scanned the answer again. Gram was someone her father respected. Maybe her grandmother
would be able to succeed where Nicole had failed.

Because the bottom line was the nanny had to
go. And if her grandmother couldn't get the job
done, then Nicole would just have to take matters
into her own hands.

* * *

They'd spent most of the morning and all of the afternoon together, but when he and Lori arrived home, Drew wasn't ready for the day to end.

When Lori thanked him for the wonderful time and turned toward the stairs, he knew he needed to act.

"Have big plans for the evening?" he asked. It was lame, but the best he could do on short notice.

Lori stopped and turned. "Actually I thought I'd go upstairs and change into something more comfortable."

Drew's heart picked up speed. He raised a brow. "Really?"

Lori laughed.

"I'm talking jogging pants and T-shirt comfortable," she said. "Not Victoria's Secret comfortable."

Victoria's Secret.

Nicole had gone there last week to buy some new pajamas. While standing out front waiting for her, Drew's eyes had been drawn to a black lace nightie in the store's window. If the baby-doll top was skimpy, the matching thong was a mere wisp of fabric....

Nicole had caught him staring at it when she'd come out of the store. Thankfully, she'd had no idea he'd been visualizing Lori in the outfit. Even now, heat raced through his veins at the thought of the black lace against Lori's bare skin.

There wasn't much fabric there at all. It wouldn't take much for a finger to hook one of those straps, lowering it...

"Drew?"

Like a splash of cold water, Lori's words doused the flames his all-too-vivid imagination had set. His gaze jerked up. "What did you say?"

"I asked if there's anything else you need before I go upstairs."

Her gaze met his and for a second Drew swore he saw a hint of amusement lurking in her eyes.

"No." He waved a dismissive hand. "You go ahead and change."

He expected Lori to head straight upstairs. Instead, she hesitated.

"You have big plans for the evening?" she asked, her hand lingering on the newel post.

"Not really." Drew shook his head. "Although I was thinking about opening a bottle of wine, maybe grabbing some cheese and crackers—"

"By yourself?"

Drew couldn't help but laugh. "I wasn't planning on being alone. I was hoping you'd join me."

"But you and I have been together all day," Lori said in a light tone.

"Is that your not-so-subtle way of saying you're sick of me?" Drew shot her a teasing smile.

"Not at all," she said immediately. "I thought it might be the other way around."

Drew didn't remember crossing the room but suddenly he was at her side, lifting her face to his. "I could never be sick of you."

Her face flushed with pleasure.

He brushed his mouth against hers, the sweetness of her lips almost his undoing.

"Go upstairs and change," he said in a voice that sounded husky even to his own ears. "I'll be in the den. Waiting."

Lori gazed at him for a long moment, her eyes so dark, they looked more brown than blue. "I'll hurry."

She flashed him a bright smile and turned to the stairs.

Drew knew it wouldn't be long until she'd be back. Which meant he didn't have a single minute to spare.

While Lori was upstairs changing, Drew had Mrs. Graham prepare a tray of cheese and crackers. He then gave her the night off.

Drew set the sterling-silver platter that overflowed with an assortment of cheeses and crackers on a table in the den, then started lighting the candles he'd confiscated from various rooms in the house.

He hoped Lori wouldn't laugh. He'd never been

much of a romantic and he wasn't sure how much ambience was too much.

By the time Lori returned, the candles were lit, the wine was chilling and soft music drifted through the room via the room's built in stereo system.

Lori broke into a delighted smile. "What's all this?"

Drew breathed a sigh of relief and lifted one shoulder in a casual shrug. "After a busy day at the Pier, I thought it might be nice for us to be able to kick back and relax."

Lori's gaze shifted from the crystal glasses to the candles then to the bottle of wine. "This is your idea of relaxing?"

For a second Drew feared he'd gone too far. Maybe it was too much.

But his doubts vanished when Lori dropped down to sit on the sofa and he saw the look in her eyes. "It's like something out of a book."

A warm glow of satisfaction filled Drew. He smiled modestly and uncorked the wine bottle. After pouring a glass for Lori and one for himself, he took a seat next to her on the sofa.

He handed her a glass and she took a sip. "This is great."

"I'm glad you like it." Drew leaned back and studied her for a moment. Not only had she changed into a clingy blue sundress, she'd put on some new perfume.

He stretched and his arm slipped around her shoulders as if it was the most natural thing in the world. "You smell really good."

She smiled and turned to face him. "It's called Pear."

"Pear?" Drew tilted his head and stared. "What kind of perfume is called Pear?"

"It's a lotion." She smiled up at him.

"Pear lotion?" Drew shook his head. "I am getting old."

"Don't start with that," Lori said, taking another sip of wine. "You're in the prime of life."

"Compared to the other guys you've dated, I'm old," he said.

Lori looked at him and for a second Drew thought she was going to tell him they *weren't* dating, that he was just her employer. But instead she smiled and shifted her gaze to the tray of food. She reached forward and grabbed a whole-wheat cracker topped with a dab of gouda.

"Actually, age isn't that important to me," she said. "It's the guy himself that matters."

Drew grabbed a cracker for himself and took another sip of wine. "What kind of man are you looking for?"

Lori paused for a moment and thoughtfully chewed her cracker. "Someone kind and compassionate. Someone fun and yet reliable. Someone who makes my heart beat faster.''

Drew finished the rest of his wine and set the glass on the table. ''Did I ever tell you I was an Eagle Scout?''

Lori's lips twitched. ''No, I don't think you ever did.''

''We help little old ladies across the street,'' Drew added.

Light dawned on Lori's face. ''Eagle Scouts are kind and compassionate—''

''No one is kinder.''

''Reliable and fun?''

''You don't get much more reliable than a Scout,'' Drew said. ''And if you've ever been to a Boy Scout jamboree you'd know we wrote the book on fun.''

''But that was a long time ago,'' Lori said in a teasing tone. ''People change. How do I know you're still all those things?''

''Did I mention Scouts are also trustworthy?''

Lori laughed and drained the last of the wine from her glass. She then leaned forward and placed the glass on the table. ''So if I ask you a question, you'll have to tell me the truth?''

Drew lifted his fingers. ''Scout's honor.''

''Do you want to kiss me as much as I want to kiss you?''

For a moment Drew thought he'd imagined

the question. After all, kissing her again had been on his mind all afternoon. But the impish twinkle in her eyes told him it hadn't been his imagination.

The enticing scent of pear filled his nostrils and the light from the candles danced across her hair. Drew lifted his hand to her face, and though the room was warm, she shivered. But when he leaned forward to kiss her, she hesitated, shifting her gaze toward the door.

"Where's Mrs. Graham?"

"I gave her the night off."

"What about Nicole? When do you think she'll be home?"

"Not for an hour at least," Drew said reassuringly. "Celia called while you were upstairs."

Her gaze met his. "You're sure?"

"Of course I am." He pulled her close. "I'm an Eagle Scout. Remember?"

She relaxed in his arms. "That's right. You're trustworthy."

"Completely," he said, lowering his mouth to hers.

He hadn't lied. She could trust him. He only wished he could trust himself. But despite his uncertainty, the minute her lips touched his, all his questions no longer seemed important.

Two years ago he'd learned that no one is

guaranteed a future. Sometimes there's just the present.

And right now he was going to enjoy every minute of it.

The candles filled the room with a golden glow. Lori wasn't sure how long they'd been kissing. The moment Drew had taken her in his arms, time had ceased to exist.

Her heart thumped noisily against her chest. Her breath came in ragged puffs.

Drew angled them so that they were nearly lying flat against the sofa cushions. His arms around her shoulders, drawing him to her.

His breathing filled her ear. He pulled her closer, his fingers lost in the thick swirl of her hair.

Lori heard herself sigh, a sound of want and need that astonished her with its intensity.

Drew's gaze met hers.

She held her breath.

The dim lights cast mysterious shadows across his lean face. His eyes glittered, suddenly looking more green and brown than blue.

She forced herself to say what they were both thinking but didn't want to admit. "We need to quit—"

Drew stopped her words, covering her mouth with his own. But this time it was a sweet kiss, gentle and soft.

"You're right," he said, softly trailing a finger down her cheek. "We do need to stop."

The words had barely passed his lips when the lights to the room snapped on.

Drew jerked up.

Lori's gaze darted to the doorway.

"Well, what have we here?" Nicole's gaze shifted from the empty wineglasses and half-burned candles to the two adults now sitting upright on the sofa. "The Nanny and the Billionaire?"

"Nicole," Mrs. Barrett snapped. "There's no need for that kind of talk."

Nicole's gaze never left Drew and Lori. "I told you how it was, Gram. Now I just hope you'll do something about it."

Chapter Thirteen

American Teen

Dear Lorelei Love,
I've worked at the local fast-food restaurant after school and on weekends since I was fifteen. My boyfriend works there, too. Except he's found someone else and now he's my ex-boyfriend. The problem is I still love him. It's really hard to work with him and pretend not to care. Unfortunately I can't afford to quit this job. They have tuition reimbursement and next year I'll need it for college.

His Ex in Hays Springs

Dear His Ex,
It's hard to be around someone you love when they don't love you back. Believe me,

I know. But you've made a commitment to your future by working at a place that can help you get an education. I applaud you for not taking the easy way out and quitting. If possible, try to get scheduled for different shifts and remember that time does make things easier. Good luck!

LL

Drew studied his mother-in-law thoughtfully. Celia hadn't said a word since Nicole and Lori had headed upstairs. Though he supposed he should be grateful, he didn't feel anything except irritation. When Celia and Nicole had appeared unexpectedly in that doorway, he'd felt like a sixteen-year-old who'd been caught with his pants down. Drew didn't like the feeling. Not at all.

He leaned back in the kitchen chair and heaved an exasperated breath. "If you've got something to say, I'd appreciate it if you'd just say it."

Celia took a long sip of coffee and peered at him over the rim of the cup. "You have to admit what was going on tonight on that sofa was inappropriate."

"I won't admit any such thing," Drew said. "Lori and I are both adults. We were just kissing, Celia. Nothing more."

"Nicole says you're sleeping with Lori."

Drew stared, not sure he'd heard correctly. "Are you joking?"

"I'm dead serious." Celia spoke matter-of-factly. "Is it true?"

Drew snorted. "I'm not even going to dignify that accusation with an answer."

Celia's unflinching gaze met his. "You were practically on top of her."

Drew bit back a harsh reply and reminded himself she only meant well. And she *was* Karen's mother. "Nothing happened."

"Would you have been able to say that if we'd come home an hour later?" Celia dropped a cube of sugar into her coffee, stirred the steaming liquid and lifted the cup to her lips.

"Yes. No. I don't know." Drew blew out a harsh breath. "Why are we having this discussion? I'm forty-three years old, not eighteen. I can take care of myself."

Celia lifted a brow. "This isn't just about you. What about Nicole? What kind of example do you think you're setting for your daughter?"

As irritated as he was at being second-guessed, Drew took a deep breath and forced himself to consider her words.

"I really like Lori," he said, knowing that was no answer, but it was the only response that came to mind.

Celia heaved an exasperated sigh, pursed her

lips and dropped one sugar cube after another into her coffee.

Drew stared. "I thought you took your coffee black."

His mother-in-law ignored the question. "God tells us to avoid situations where we can be tempted."

"Give me a break, Celia," Drew said, his tone harsher than he'd intended. "Joe hasn't been gone that long. Don't tell me you've forgotten what it's like to want that closeness?"

"Of course I haven't forgotten." Celia's gentle tone only made Drew feel worse. "But making love belongs in marriage, after two people have made a commitment to each other and to God. Are you and Lori talking about marriage?"

Marry Lori? The idea took Drew by surprise. He liked her and respected her. But marriage hadn't entered his mind.

"Lori and I are just friends. That's all." Drew spoke with special emphasis so there would be no misunderstanding.

"Then you'd better think twice about spending so much time on the couch. Or you might find yourself forced into a marriage you don't want."

"What do you mean by that crack?"

"You're a wealthy man, Drew," Celia said. "Lori seems like a nice young woman, but Nicole is sure she's after your money."

"What do you think?" Drew's voice sounded strained even to his own ears.

Celia dropped yet another cube of sugar into her coffee. "I think she may be right."

Lori's hand stilled on the door to the kitchen. She'd only come downstairs for a glass of milk. She'd had no idea Celia and Drew would still be up talking.

Nicole is sure she's after your money.

Hot anger flowed through Lori's veins. How dare Nicole say such a thing? She'd love Drew McCashlin even if he didn't have a penny to his name.

Love Drew McCashlin? Lori's breath caught in her throat and she leaned against the doorway, the realization so overwhelming. After all these years, she was finally in love.

But how could that be? A middle-aged Eagle Scout with three children wasn't at all what she had in mind.

I'm loyal, trustworthy, kind...

Lori smiled as Drew's words came rushing back. Though she'd given him a hard time, she knew he was all those things and more.

She remembered his kindness to Molly, the way his eyes glowed with love and pride whenever he talked about Clay and Nicole, and the gentle consideration he'd always showed her. How could a woman *not* love such a man?

Lori and I are just friends. That's all.

Lori listened in growing shock to the rest of the conversation, her heart hammering against her chest. Not only did Nicole think she was a money-grubbing schemer, Mrs. Barrett concurred. And Drew was uncharacteristically silent. Surely he didn't think his daughter and mother-in-law were right?

Her chest tightened. Anybody in Shelby could tell him that Lori Loveland was as honest as they come. But unfortunately she wasn't in Shelby and nobody in Chicago could vouch for her character.

She angrily brushed a tear from her eye. Why did she need someone to vouch for her anyway? If Drew didn't know her better than that…

Lori took a deep steadying breath. She wanted nothing more than to yank open the kitchen door and tell Drew and his mother-in-law just what she thought of the ridiculous allegations. But years of curbing such impulsivity along with the knowledge that nothing would be accomplished by the action made Lori pull her hand from the doorknob.

Before she could change her mind, Lori turned on her heel and headed for the stairs. The best thing would be for her to go back to bed and forget everything she'd heard tonight.

Tomorrow would be soon enough to decide how to deal with being in love with a man who didn't love her.

Nicole sat in the chair next to her bed and flipped through the magazine she'd "borrowed" from her grandmother's house. But she couldn't keep her mind on any of the articles. All she could think of was her father and grandmother. If only she could be a fly on the kitchen wall.

Despite Nicole's warning, her grandmother had been shocked to find her son-in-law on the sofa with the nanny. Though Gram hadn't said a word, her cheeks had turned bright red and her eyes had been wide as saucers.

Nicole had only been disappointed they still had their feet on the floor. Personally, it would have been much more effective if her grandmother would have caught the two in bed together having their "torrid" affair. Her father couldn't have denied his actions if he'd been caught in the act.

Unfortunately right now he was probably downstairs assuring her grandmother that he and the nanny had only exchanged a few kisses. By the time he finished, her grandmother would be apologizing for doubting his integrity.

Nicole snorted. *What a hypocrite.* Both of her parents had always preached abstinence as the only choice before marriage. Obviously her father had reconsidered and decided that wasn't the only option. At least not for him.

And he hadn't even known Lori as long as Nicole had known Justin. And Nicole had never slept with him.

Nicole sighed, her fingers moving up to her neck to the heart-shaped locket Justin had given her for Valentine's Day. He was so sweet, so caring. And he loved her.

Justin had told her he wanted their relationship to move to the "next level." So far she'd been able to keep their physical relationship confined to kisses at the end of the evening. And she'd deliberately avoided tempting situations such as the boy-girl camp-out earlier in the summer and the spring break trip to Cancún. Not that her dad would have let her go if he'd known these were coed activities with no chaperone, but he wouldn't have had to know. Kids at her school considered lying to be an art and they usually got away with it.

But Nicole had never liked deceiving her dad. Because he'd always been up-front with her. At least, until Lori Loveland had showed up.

If only Mom were here.

Nicole's heart clenched. If her mother hadn't gone and died, none of this would be happening. Blinking back unexpected tears, Nicole swiped her eyes with the back of her hand.

She missed talking to her mother, asking her opinion. Gram was nice, but she was old. If Nicole were ever foolish enough to mention she was considering sleeping with her boyfriend, she had no doubt her grandmother would drop dead on the spot.

A heartfelt sigh escaped Nicole's lips and her gaze dropped to the magazine in her lap. If only she had an older sister—someone cool like Lorelei Love—that knew the score to give her some advice.

Nicole thought for a moment, an idea taking shape in her head. Reaching over, she pulled her laptop off the bed and popped it open. Although some of the girls at school insisted the letters in advice columns were made up, Nicole believed they came from actual readers. And though she didn't want her letter to end up in the magazine, she'd love to know Lorelei's opinion.

Nicole clicked on her alternate e-mail address—the one none of her friends would recognize—and started typing.

Dear Lorelei Love,
My boyfriend and I have been dating for over six months. Will is a cool guy and very popular. All my friends tell me I'm lucky to have him. I tell them he's lucky to have me. But the truth is, I do feel lucky to have such a

wonderful boyfriend. Plenty of other girls at school would take my place in a minute.

So what's the problem?

Although he says he loves me, I'm not sure he really does or if he's just saying it because that's what you say to a girl you're kissing. Anyway, he wants to have sex, and although he's been cool about it, I can tell he's getting tired of taking no for an answer.

I don't want to lose him, but something is stopping me from saying yes.

My friends say go for it. That you have to lose your virginity sometime and it might as well be with someone as good-looking as him. What do you think?

                                        Mia

P.S. Is there any way you could just e-mail me your answer?

Nicole spell-checked the letter, took a deep breath and hit Send. She'd disguised her situation as much as she could—changing Justin's name to Will and her own to Mia. Hopefully if her letter did make it into the magazine, those changes would be enough to keep anyone from guessing she wrote it.

That was, assuming Lorelei Love even existed. And, if she did, that she answered the letters she received.

* * *

Though Lori was tired when she returned to her room, sleep eluded her. She opened her Bible and read for several minutes. But tonight even her favorite passages couldn't still her restlessness. There was so much to think about, so many decisions to make.

After Celia Barrett got through with him, would Drew want her gone? And if she had to leave tomorrow, where would she go?

But if she ended up staying, how could she face him every day knowing she loved him and he didn't love her in return?

Lori's hand rose to knead her tense neck muscles. She had to start thinking about something else or she'd never get to sleep.

Her gaze drifted to her computer. It had been several days since she'd last checked her Lorelei Love e-mail. The magazine's computer system automatically forwarded her the letters she received and she was always eager to read and answer the questions.

Maybe reading about someone else's troubles would help take her mind off her own....

Lori signed on and went straight to her e-mail account. The questions in this batch appeared to be fairly typical: school, boyfriend and parent problems. Lori read through them with well-practiced ease, looking for those reflecting the topics the editors had suggested she focus on for the next issue.

One by one she scanned the letters, searching out the ones she needed to answer first. She was just about to close out the last one when a name at the bottom of the list caught her eye.

Mia.

She had to chuckle. Lori hadn't thought about Mia in years. Mia had been the name of her best friend in junior high. The girl she'd known all those years ago may have moved from Shelby in eighth grade, but Lori had never forgotten her.

Lori stared at the screen, knowing the letter's premarital sex question wasn't a good fit for the next issue. But there was something about the letter that made her pause. Something that touched her heart. Something that made her *want* to answer it personally.

But *American Teen* guidelines warned against answering e-mails personally. Their rationale for the rule made complete sense. It was best for any responses to come through a controlled venue.

But there was something about Mia's e-mail....

Lori read it again, more slowly this time. Whether it was the name or the postscript that made her pause, Lori didn't know. All she knew was this was one e-mail she had to answer.

Dear Mia,
Thanks for writing. It's not easy to share your feelings with a stranger. I know because it's

equally hard to give advice to someone you don't know. That's why I'm hoping you wouldn't mind telling me a little bit about yourself.

I'm not asking for any deep dark secrets, just basic stuff, like: How old are you? Do you live with both your parents? Do you have any brothers or sisters? Do you have a religious faith?

I look forward to hearing from you.

Lorelei Love

P.S. My best friend in junior high was named Mia.

Nicole had just finished sending an e-mail to her friend Erin when she noticed she had new mail.

Excitement coursed up her spine at the sight of the return address. She clicked on the letter and read the text, unable to believe she'd gotten such a quick response. A smile touched her lips at Lorelei Love's P.S.

It was crazy, she knew, but Nicole couldn't help but feel better already. She couldn't help but think she and Lorelei Love were destined to become friends.

How cool would that be?

Chapter Fourteen

American Teen

Dear Lorelei Love,
My life sucks. I had a great future in soccer until I blew out my knee. Surgery didn't work for me. I'm a senior and unable to do what I love most. To make matters worse, all of my friends were ''soccer friends.'' Since we don't have that in common I'm all alone. What can I do?

Hating Life in Houston

Dear Hating Life,
What a bummer to have your soccer career cut short. But just because you can't play anymore doesn't mean you can't still be in-

volved in the sport. You could be a team manager, a coach or even just a fan. Or you could decide to do something totally different. Life is full of wonderful new opportunities if we just open our eyes and look around. I firmly believe that when one door closes, another one opens. So, start looking for that open door!

LL

"Mr. McCashlin?"

Drew looked up from his computer screen. His secretary stood in the office doorway, her purse already over her shoulder, a pair of sunglasses held loosely in one hand. "Yes?"

"I'm getting ready to leave for the day. Is there anything you need before I go?"

Drew waved a dismissive hand. "It can wait until morning."

Drew had to smile at her relieved expression. Amanda had recently become engaged and the extra money she earned working late no longer seemed to hold much appeal.

"Have a good evening, then." She flashed him a brilliant smile and was gone before he could say another word.

Leaning back in his chair, Drew shifted his gaze once again to the computer screen. He stared unblinking at the rows of numbers for several minutes before shutting down the program.

Normally he liked reviewing cost reports and other financial data, but right now he couldn't think of anything but what his mother-in-law had said last night.

Celia was right. He *was* playing with fire. He'd always prided himself on being a logical man. When he'd built his business he'd evaluated his options, had developed long- and short-term business plans and had stuck with them. And because he'd never let his emotions sway his decisions, he'd been successful.

But his relationship with Lori hadn't been part of any long- or short-term plan, it had just happened. Certainly the attraction had been there from the beginning. But he'd been dating Susan, and Lori had Tom, so he'd assumed that's all it would be—an attraction. Then he and Susan had parted ways and Tom left the picture, as well.

Drew stood and raked his fingers through his hair. What had he been thinking asking Lori out to dinner? And why hadn't he just said he would take Molly to the Navy Pier himself?

Because you weren't thinking, that's why. You were going on emotion.

And the truth was, he liked Lori. She was fun and upbeat and when he was with her, he felt like a kid again. That's what had gotten him in trouble in the first place. He was a father, not a kid, and any decisions he made about having a woman in his life had to be made with that fact in mind.

Even he could see Lori was totally wrong for him. She was young, just starting out in life. In time she'd probably want to settle down and get married, maybe have a couple of kids. At one time he'd wanted more children—but Karen's hysterectomy after Molly's birth had put an end to those dreams. Now he was getting too old.

An image of a little boy with Lori's big blue eyes flashed before him. He shoved it aside.

There was no future in a relationship with Lori. And the sooner his heart realized it, the better.

Lori closed her Bible with a sigh. She'd always thought she knew what she'd wanted out of life. Now she wasn't so sure.

A few months ago, she'd gotten a new job, a new place to live and a new boyfriend. The life she'd always dreamed of was hers for the taking.

But somewhere along the line, what she wanted had changed. The idea of partying no longer held the appeal it once did. She'd rather spend a quiet evening with Drew, listening to jazz or relaxing in front of a fire, sharing a bottle of wine.

And she was ready to be a mother. She already loved little Molly, and though she and Nicole weren't exactly best buds, she'd been around teens enough to know that the situation could change overnight. And the fact remained, they were part of Drew. How could she not love them?

But in the end it didn't matter, because for she and Drew to go the distance, love had to be a two-way street.

All day she'd rehearsed in her head what she was going to say when she saw him. She'd briefly considered being truthful and telling him what she'd overheard and how that made her feel, but had quickly discarded that idea. He'd already made his feelings quite clear when he'd told his mother-in-law they were just friends.

A part of her would like nothing more than to pack her bags and walk out the door. But she'd made a commitment to Drew. And to the girls.

Though Lori was sure Nicole wouldn't bat an eye at her leaving, Molly would be devastated. And the last thing she wanted was to rock Molly's world.

If Lori had to swallow her pride and pretend her heart wasn't breaking in two, so that Molly could continue to feel safe and secure, that's just what she'd do.

She closed her eyes and her thoughts drifted heavenward.

God, why You let me fall in love with Drew McCashlin I'll never know. But You did and now I need Your help. Please help me to say and do the right thing so that no one gets hurt. Thank You. Amen.

So that no one gets hurt.

Lori's heart twisted. Who was she kidding? Even God couldn't perform that miracle.

Because for her, a broken heart was virtually guaranteed.

By the time Drew finally got home from work it was after nine. Mrs. Graham met him at the door on her way out and told him there was food in the refrigerator. He thanked her, then lied and told her he'd already eaten.

The truth was he had no appetite. Just the thought of telling Lori that they should keep their relationship strictly business made him feel sick. But it had to be done. It had been a mistake for them to get so close. At this rate it wouldn't be long before he'd be crazy in love with her. In fact, he already suspected that was the case.

"Drew?"

He shifted his gaze to the stairs. Lori stood on the first landing. His breath caught in his throat.

Dressed in a white skirt and matching sleeveless top, Lori looked like a radiant angel. Her blond hair hung loose to her shoulders and her blue eyes appeared large and luminous in her beautiful face. "Do you have a minute?"

The lump in the pit of his stomach hardened into a tight knot.

"Sure." Drew forced a casual tone. "What's up?"

She glided down the stairs with a grace he couldn't help but admire. At the bottom, her gaze shifted in the direction of the den. "Maybe we could sit down?"

The image of her on the sofa flashed through his mind. The remembrance so vivid he could practically smell her lotion and feel her silky hair against his face. What he wouldn't give to have her in his arms again....

Drew took a deep steadying breath and thought quickly. "I haven't eaten dinner yet," he said. "Why don't you join me in the kitchen? That is, if you don't mind if I eat while we talk?"

The offer came out casual and offhand, just as he'd hoped. If they had to speak one-on-one, he preferred the hard wooden chairs and brightly lit kitchen to the cozy den and overstuffed couch.

"Of course I don't mind," Lori said softly.

They walked to the kitchen and Drew held the door open for Lori. He followed her into the room, letting the door shut behind him. "Are the girls in bed?"

"Nicole is spending the night with Lisa," Lori said. "And Molly fell asleep not more than twenty minutes ago."

"How *was* Nicole this evening?" Drew opened the refrigerator door and glanced inside, not the least bit interested in the shelves of food. "I didn't get a chance to talk to her before I went to work."

"I barely saw her myself." Lori took a seat at the table. "She and Lisa had some special cheer-leading practice today. Then Lisa's mother called around five and asked if Nicole could spend the night."

"How did Molly's day go?"

Lori's lips curved in a smile and her tense expression relaxed. "Molly had a great day."

"Did she say anything?" Drew straightened and shut the refrigerator door. He turned back to Lori, giving her his full attention. "Any sound? Any words?"

"Believe me, if she'd have talked I would have been on that phone to you in a heartbeat," Lori said.

Though the news was what he'd expected, Drew couldn't stop the tide of disappointment that washed over him.

"It'll happen," Lori said with that quiet confidence he admired.

"I hope so," Drew replied.

He took a seat at the table and an awkward silence descended. "What did you two do today?"

"Molly and I drove over to Elgin. We had lunch

then we went to a bookstore where one of Molly's favorite authors was doing a book-signing.''

It was a typical mother-daughter activity. Drew's heart twisted. ''I bet she liked that.''

''Now I know you didn't ask me in here to talk about Molly,'' Lori said. Her eyes were filled with an emotion Drew couldn't quite identify.

''I seem to remember you're the one who wanted to speak with me,'' Drew said lightly.

''You forget. We're on the same wavelength,'' Lori said. ''Something is on your mind.''

When Drew had analyzed their relationship and decided on his course of action, Lori hadn't been right in front of him, looking so beautiful. She took his breath away. The words he needed to say stuck in his throat.

''About last night…'' she ventured finally when he remained silent.

''Actually, I want to apologize for that,'' Drew answered. ''Things got a little out of hand.''

Lori's gaze was solemn. ''All we did was kiss.''

''I hope Nicole believes that.'' Drew heaved a frustrated sigh.

''I've been thinking about the whole situation,'' Lori said softly. ''Although we didn't do anything wrong, it certainly looked questionable. I think it's a mistake for us to get so involved.''

Hearing the words come from her was so un-expected, for a second Drew wasn't sure he'd heard correctly. ''You think our relationship is a mistake?''

She met his gaze, a sadness lingering in her eyes. ''There's never going to be anything permanent between us. We both know that. That's why I don't think it's wise for us to kiss anymore.''

''Finding me a little too hard to resist?'' he asked in a joking tone. Though he'd planned on telling her the same thing, hearing the words from her lips still stung.

Lori laughed. ''As a matter of fact…yes.''

Drew couldn't stop the flash of pleasure that coursed through him at her words. His gaze remained on her lips. Why was it when the conversation was headed in the right direction did he suddenly have the urge to go in the other direction?

''But physical attraction isn't everything,'' she added as if she could read his thoughts.

''Are you saying that's all you feel for me?'' Drew didn't know why he was pressing the point. If he were smart, he'd just agree and let it end here.

''Don't play games with me, Drew.'' Lori's voice, though soft, had a hard edge. She pushed back her chair and stood. ''You know very well how powerful such feelings can be. That's why I think it's best if we kept our relationship strictly business.''

Drew reluctantly nodded, knowing it was for the best. Heck, it was what he'd wanted.

But even as he agreed, what Drew couldn't understand was how something so right could feel so wrong.

"And that's it," Drew said, sitting back in the booth.

He'd called first thing in the morning and arranged to pick Nicole up from her friend's house. She'd been silent during the drive to a nearby restaurant. Though the small café's chocolate-chip pancakes were Nicole's favorite, she'd refused to order anything but a tall glass of juice.

Sipping the frothy orange liquid from a straw, Nicole stared at Drew from beneath lowered lashes. "So you're telling me the affair is over?"

Drew's jaw tightened. Hadn't she heard a word he'd said? "There never was an affair. I told you that."

"She said you slept together." Nicole lifted her chin and met his gaze, a faint splash of color dotting her cheeks.

"Well, if she said that she was lying," Drew said, keeping his temper under control and his tone matter of fact.

Nicole tossed her head. "Why would she lie?"

"I don't know." Drew heaved an exasperated sigh. "The point is nothing happened. And nothing is going to happen. Lori and I talked and we both decided it would be best if we kept our relationship strictly business.''

Nicole's gaze widened. "For real?"

Drew nodded. "For real."

"Oh, Daddy," Nicole squealed, and reached across the table to give him a hug. "I'm so happy."

Drew forced a smile, glad someone could be happy. Because he was perfectly miserable.

Dear Lorelei Love,

Thanks for writing back! I think us getting to know each other better is a fab idea.

I'll start first. I'm sixteen. I live with my dad and two brothers. My mom left us a couple of years ago. She won't be coming back. I miss her, but at least I have my dad.

Dad is a cool guy, though he can be bossy at times. And occasionally stupid. Like when he was dating this woman who was so wrong for him. Thankfully my heavy-duty praying paid off. He told me today they'd broken up!

But back to my problem with Kevin. What do you think? Should I sleep with him or not?

Your friend,

Mia

Lori stared at her computer screen. For some odd reason, Mia reminded her of Nicole. Maybe it was because she had no doubt Nicole would be thrilled when she heard she and Drew were no longer together.

She sighed. None of them would probably even miss her when she was gone. And in time Drew would find a woman to share his life, someone Nicole would tolerate and Molly would adore. Someone who liked listening to jazz and riding Ferris wheels. Someone he could love, who'd love him back.

But he has that woman now. He has me.

When she'd told him they should keep their relationship strictly business she'd expected him to argue, to put up a fight, to tell her it was a bad idea. Instead, after a halfhearted protest, he'd agreed.

She'd told herself it was for the best. That he wasn't what she wanted anyway. But Lori knew she was just lying to herself. She might be able to hide her feelings from Drew, but she couldn't hide them from herself.

She brushed aside the self-pitying tears that threatened to spill and turned her attention back to the screen. It wasn't until she'd finished her e-mail and sent it that she realized Mia's boyfriend's name had changed from Will to Kevin.

Lori had to chuckle. Mia had obviously changed the name of her boyfriend to protect his identity…and her own. It was such a common occurrence in the letters Lori received that she usually didn't give it a second thought. But now she couldn't help but wonder if the girl who called herself Mia had another name, as well.

Lori sat on the edge of her bed and reached for a strappy sandal. It had been a long week. Molly hadn't uttered another sound, and true to his word, Drew had kept his distance. And she and Nicole were polite and distant strangers.

Though Lori prayed every night for strength and guidance, her soul remained troubled. She still couldn't understand why God had let her fall in love with a man who didn't love her.

A knock pulled her from her reverie. She stood and crossed the room, opening the door.

Dressed in her Sunday best, Molly stood in the doorway holding a ponytail holder and a ribbon in her outstretched hand.

Lori couldn't help but smile. "I take it you're in the mood to have your hair up?"

Molly nodded shyly.

"Come on in." Lori stepped aside to let the child enter. "I'll grab a brush."

It only took a minute to secure Molly's hair. Getting the ribbon just right took a little longer.

"Beautiful." Lori stepped back to admire her work.

"That's just what I was thinking."

Lori turned and for the first time noticed Drew leaning against the doorjamb, his arms crossed, his gaze firmly fixed on her. Lori's heart picked up speed, but she ignored his comment. Instead she turned her attention back to Molly. "I think you and I are ready for church."

"Good," Drew said. "I'll bring the car around front."

Lori frowned and reluctantly shifted her gaze. Not only was Drew up early, he had on a navy suit—one so dark it almost looked black—with a crisp white shirt and a tie she recognized as a Valentino. "Are you going in to work today?"

Drew laughed. "I don't work on Sunday."

Lori paused. "Then why are you all dressed up?"

"Because I'm going to church," he said, giving Molly a quick wink.

Molly smiled with delight and ran across the room into his arms.

"Th-that's wonderful," Lori stammered. She'd encouraged him to come along, but she'd never expected him to comply.

"Church starts in twenty minutes." Nicole's voice sounded from down the hall. "I don't care when we leave, but I'm telling you right now I'm not walking in late."

Nicole paused in the doorway, her eyes widening at the sight of her father in Lori's bedroom.

The sudden tightness in her jaw eased when she saw her sister.

"Your father has decided to come to church with us," Lori said. "Isn't that great?"

Not only did Nicole ignore Lori's question, the teen didn't even glance in her direction. Her gaze remained focused on her father. "Since you're going, does that mean we can leave the nanny at home?"

Chapter Fifteen

American Teen

Dear Lorelei Love,
Last week my schnauzer, Hans, died. He was a wonderful dog and I loved him so much.

My parents have already started talking about getting another dog. So far I've said absolutely not. The way I look at it, no dog can replace Hans. But I'm afraid my parents don't see it that way.

Grieving in Galveston

Dear Grieving,
First, let me express my condolences on Hans' death. It is never easy to lose someone you love.

Though you might not be ready for another dog just yet, eventually you will be ready to love again. You'll see a little ball of fur with a wet tongue and your heart will go pitter patter. No dog will ever replace Hans and you'll never forget him, but you will love again. Trust me on this one.

LL

Years ago Lori had fallen off her bike. The impact had been sudden and unexpected. She felt the same way now.

When Lori had thought about Drew accompanying them to church, she'd never imagined that meant *she* wouldn't go.

Lori took a deep steadying breath and tried to look at it from Nicole's point of view. After all, in the teen's mind, Lori was just a chauffeur, no more. No less.

"Nicole's right," Lori said quickly, earning a surprised look from the teen. "You three go on without me."

Drew opened his mouth to protest but Molly spoke first.

"No." Molly shook her head and clasped Lori's hand tight. "You come, too."

Lori's breath caught in her throat. Though Molly had spoken softly, the words had been clearly audible.

Drew's face paled.

Nicole stared at her sister, a stunned expression on her face.

Drew moved to Molly's side and crouched down beside her.

"You talked," he said in a husky tone, his voice filled with wonder.

Molly ducked her head and buried her face in the skirt of Lori's dress. Lori's hand moved supportively to the girl's shoulder.

Lori drew a shuddering breath and closed her eyes, overwhelmed by emotion. *Thank You, God. Thank You so much.*

Lori opened her eyes to find the three of them staring.

"Are you ready to go?" Drew asked.

Lori hesitated, her gaze shifting to Nicole.

The teen's eyes were shiny and though she didn't smile, the antagonism that had filled her gaze only a moment earlier was absent.

"Come if you want." The teen lifted one shoulder in a slight shrug. "But we'd better hurry because—"

"—you're not walking in late," Drew and Lori finished the sentence together.

Molly giggled. Even Nicole couldn't help but crack a smile.

Though Molly didn't speak again during the ride to church, they were all in a lighthearted mood when they walked through the church's front door.

Drew and Lori slid into a pew close to the front, the two girls between them. Lori half expected Nicole to pull out her Palm Pilot the minute the sermon started, but the teen kept her eyes firmly fixed on the minister. And when the prayers were said, Nicole even folded her hands and bowed her head with the rest of the congregation.

Lori was struck by the sudden intimacy of it all. The sunlight streaming in through the stained-glass windows, the familiar music bursting from the pipe organ, the little girl snuggled up tight against her. This was the life she wanted. Not partying until dawn in some smoke-filled dance club. Why had it taken her so long to realize what was truly important?

Filled with a feeling she found difficult to control, Lori leaned over and pressed a kiss against the top of Molly's head.

When Lori lifted her head, her gaze was drawn to the cross. God knew what was best for her. She simply had to trust in Him. It was what she should have done all along.

She thought of all her prayers this past year. Instead of praying that God's will be done, she'd put in her order, telling the Almighty exactly the type of man she wanted and didn't want.

Maybe God wasn't giving her Drew because He was planning to give her exactly what she'd asked for: a single, never-married Christian man. It was a sobering thought and it brought to mind one of her mother's old sayings: Be Careful What You Wish For, It Just May Come True.

Lori had never really understood the adage.

It hadn't made sense.

Until now.

Nicole reread the bio Lorelei Love had sent her, reviewing every detail. According to this information, the columnist wasn't much older than her brother. Too bad Clay was already married or Nicole could have hooked them up. It would have been great having a woman like Lorelei be a part of the family.

In the last couple of weeks, she and Lorelei had exchanged numerous e-mails, discussing a variety of topics. Nicole had grown to like and respect the woman. Though Lorelei didn't always tell her what she wanted to hear, the columnist always seemed to have good rationale for her opinion.

It was strange. At thirty, Lorelei could be a mother herself, but the way she worded her "advice" was more like an older sister. Lorelei never came out and directly said, "Don't do that." She "suggested" alternatives.

Like with Justin. Just "talking" with Lorelei had helped Nicole realize she wasn't ready to be intimate with him. Though she wasn't sure she was willing to do as Lorelei suggested and wait until she was married to make love, Nicole had decided to keep things low-key for now.

She agreed with Lorelei. If Justin truly loved her, he wouldn't break up with her just because she said no. And if he did leave, what would she have lost?

Having Lorelei available to bounce ideas off was almost like having a mother again. Only, of course Lorelei was a lot younger. And way more cool than any mother.

Nicole sighed. For a long time she'd been convinced it would be a mistake for her father to marry again. But now she wasn't so sure if that hadn't been selfish. In a few years she'd be away at college. Who would Molly have to talk to about the day-to-day girl things then? Dad was great, but he was still a man.

Maybe her attitude *had* been short-sighted. Maybe having a stepmom might be okay. Maybe, instead of complaining about the women in her Dad's life, she should be out there doing some matchmaking.

Nicole stared at the screen and wondered if she'd ever be able to find someone like Lorelei Love for her father.

Lori took a sip of chai and smiled at her best friend. "I'm so glad you called."

Kaitlyn Killeen McCashlin wrapped her fingers

around her steaming latte, the huge diamond on her left hand casting fiery sparks in the bistro's dim light.

With her thick auburn hair and cat-green eyes, Kaitlyn had always been a beautiful woman, but today she looked positively radiant.

"Marriage suits you," Lori said. "I don't think I've ever seen you look happier."

"That's because I've never been happier," Kaitlyn said, a tiny smile tugging at the corners of her lips. "Especially after the news I got today."

"Don't stop there." Lori sat up straight. "Tell me everything."

When Kaitlyn had called her out of the blue this morning and asked her to lunch, Lori suspected something was up. And when she'd asked Lori not to mention to Drew or the girls that she was in town, Lori was sure of it. Now it looked like her suspicions were well-founded.

"You know how I told you I was here on business?" Kaitlyn asked. "Well, that's what I told Clay, too. But that's not quite the truth."

"So…tell me," Lori urged, finding Kaitlyn's obvious excitement contagious.

"I came here to see my doctor," Kaitlyn said. "You know how it is in Shelby. You walk into Doc Edwards's office and everyone knows why you were there before you're even out the door."

"A doctor?" Lori's heart tightened. "Are you sick?"

"No." A sudden grin covered Kaitlyn's face. "I'm pregnant."

Lori squealed and reached across the table, giving her friend a big hug. "Kaitlyn, that is so great. I'm so happy for you."

"I'm happy, too," Kaitlyn said.

"Then why the secrecy?" Puzzled, Lori tilted her head. "If I was married and pregnant I'd be shouting it from the rooftops. I'd want everyone to know."

"I *do* want everyone to know. *After* I tell Clay." Kaitlyn's smile turned rueful. "But I had to tell you. Once the doctor confirmed my suspicions, I felt like I'd go crazy if I didn't tell someone. And I want to tell Clay in person, not over the phone."

"Tell me again why he didn't come with you."

"He wanted to," Kaitlyn said. "But I told him I'd be in meetings all day. I didn't want to get his hopes up if it turned out to be a false alarm."

"I'm so glad you called me," Lori said. "And I promise, I won't say a word about this to Drew."

"Drew?" Kaitlyn lifted a brow, her eyes bright with interest.

"I mean Mr. McCashlin." Lori could feel her face warm. So far she'd kept her feelings about Kaitlyn's father-in-law to herself. It was humiliating enough to fall in love with your boss, without everyone knowing he didn't return the feelings.

"No, you don't." Kaitlyn's eyes sparkled with curiosity. "You meant Drew. Something is going on between the two of you and you're going to tell me all about it."

"Nothing is going on." Unexpectedly Lori's voice broke. "Nothing."

Kaitlyn's gaze narrowed. "What happened? What did he do?"

Lori took a steadying breath and waved a dismissive hand. "It's nothing, really. I fell in love with him and the only thing he did was not love me back."

The words came out casual and offhand, just as she'd intended. Lori had thought she'd pulled it off, but Kaitlyn knew her too well.

"Oh, Lori, I'm so sorry." Kaitlyn's eyes filled with concern. "How could anyone not love you? Anyone can see the two of you would be perfect together."

Lori lifted one shoulder in a slight shrug. "He just wants to be friends."

"Friends?" Kaitlyn rolled her eyes. "Has the guy got rocks in his head or what?"

"Careful," Lori said in a light tone. "Remember, that's your child's grandfather you're talking about."

"I know, and I adore him," Kaitlyn said. "But this doesn't make any sense."

"Since when does life make any sense?" Lori gave a little laugh. "It seems like just when you think you've got things figured out—"

"Lori?"

Lori's breath caught in her throat at the sound of the all-too-familiar voice. She heard Kaitlyn gasp. Slowly Lori shifted her gaze sideways.

Dressed in her favorite charcoal-gray suit, Drew stood in the aisle with another businessman at his side. Lori recognized the man from the party at Tom's house. She forced a welcoming smile. "Mr. McCashlin. Mr. Claron. What a surprise."

"Hello, Drew," Kaitlyn said in a perfectly composed voice.

Drew's gaze, which had been riveted to Lori, shifted across the table. His eyes widened. "Kaitlyn? I didn't notice…I mean, what are you doing in Chicago? Is Clay with you?"

"Clay's back in Shelby," Kaitlyn said. "I just flew in for the day. I had some…appointments."

If Drew noticed his daughter-in-law's slight hesitation, he didn't mention it. "I'm surprised you didn't call."

Hugh Claron gave Lori a friendly smile before his curious gaze settled on Kaitlyn. "I take it you're Clay's wife."

"I'm sorry, Hugh. I thought you knew my

daughter-in-law,'' Drew said. ''I forgot you had to miss the wedding.''

Drew made quick work of the introductions.

''How is your father?'' The look Hugh Claron shot Kaitlyn was filled with genuine concern. ''Drew mentioned he'd had some sort of surgery recently.''

Lori hid a smile. The older gentleman's question prevented Drew from quizzing Kaitlyn further about the reason for her visit. When the hostess told the two men their table was ready, Lori heaved a sigh of relief.

''Whew.'' Lori shook her head. ''What are the odds we'd run into Drew?''

''I'm glad we did,'' Kaitlyn said. ''I got all my questions answered.''

''What questions?'' Lori asked.

Kaitlyn's lips pursed together in a satisfied smile. ''When you told me Drew didn't love you, I couldn't see how that could be. Now it makes sense.''

''It does.''

''At least some of it does,'' Kaitlyn said. ''He loves you—that I'm sure of. The only thing I can't understand is why he hasn't told you.''

''Tell me again why she was in town?'' Drew asked.

Lori noted he'd waited until they were in the

middle of eating dinner to pose the question that had been hovering on his lips since she'd walked in the door.

She could see why Drew had been such a success in business. He'd bided his time and waited for the perfect opportunity to strike. After all, it was now impossible for Lori to blithely toss off some comment and leave the room.

"She had some appointments." Lori shifted her gaze to Molly. "Did you want any more chicken?"

"What kind of appointments?" Drew pressed when Molly shook her head.

Lori took a sip of water and shrugged. "Kaitlyn didn't say."

"Kaitlyn was in town?" Nicole lowered her fork. "Why didn't she stop by and see us?"

"That's what I'm trying to determine," Drew said.

"Sir?" Mrs. Graham appeared in the doorway. "Your son is on the phone. He says it's important that he speak with you right away."

A worried frown creased Drew's brow. He pushed his chair back from the table and stood. "I'll take the call in the den."

Nicole and Molly exchanged worried glances.

"Don't worry, girls," Lori said. "I think your brother just has some good news he wants to share."

Kaitlyn had a husband she loved, a career as a

fashion designer that was challenging and fulfilling and now she would have a baby. Lori sighed. Some girls just had all the luck.

Though the evening air held a hint of chill, Lori was perfectly comfortable on the porch swing dressed in jeans and a bulky University of Iowa sweatshirt.

After Drew had returned to the table with the good news, Lori had tried to get into the festive atmosphere. But by the end of the meal, she had a headache from the effort. She'd passed on dessert and excused herself.

It wasn't that she wasn't happy for Clay and Kaitlyn, it was just that it was hard to feel like celebrating when your own love life was in the toilet.

"I wondered where you'd gone." Drew stepped out onto the back porch and pulled the door shut behind him.

"I'm just a little tired tonight."

Drew took a seat in the wicker chair opposite Lori. "You knew she was pregnant."

Lori shrugged, a tiny smile lifting her lips. "She was so excited, she just couldn't keep the news to herself. But she really wanted Clay to be the first to know."

"He's thrilled."

"I'm sure he is," Lori said, hating herself for

not being more enthusiastic. After all, these two people were her friends.

"What's the matter, Lori?" Drew asked in a soft voice.

Maybe it was the darkness. Or the gentle concern in his voice. Or the fact that she was suddenly so incredibly tired of pretending.

"I'm jealous."

"Jealous?"

At any other time the look on his face would have been comical.

"I'm five years older than Kaitlyn. Five years, Drew." Lori raked her fingers through her hair. "Yet Kaitlyn is the one that's married. And *she's* the one having the baby. It should be me."

The sentiment sounded worse said aloud.

"Forget I said anything." Embarrassed at her outburst, Lori started to rise, but Drew grabbed her arm, pulling her back down. She turned her face from him. "I'm a horrible person for even thinking such thoughts."

"Well, if you are," Drew said, "then so am I."

Whatever response she'd expected from him, it wasn't this. Lori looked at him in surprise. "I don't understand."

"Karen and I always wanted a big family, five or six kids at least. I know it's a crazy notion, especially in this age of overpopulation," he said. "Still, when Clay was telling me the news, I found

myself wishing it was me that was going to be a
father again. If I had a second chance, there'd be
so many things I'd do differently.''

''I don't see what,'' Lori said. ''You're a wonderful father. And you've got three great children.
You know how I feel about Clay. And Nicole is
an incredible young lady—so passionate and intense, so full of life. I admit she can be a bit obstinate at times, but I have to admit I like her
spunk. And Molly....''

Hidden in the evening shadows, Nicole eased
the door shut and stepped back into the house. Lori
and her father had been so intent on their conversation they hadn't even heard the door open.

I like her spunk.

The words both surprised Nicole and warmed
her heart. Ever since she'd been a little girl she'd
been outspoken, what many would call a ''strong-
willed child.'' At times that strong will had driven
her mother crazy. Although her mom had always
said she loved her children equally, Nicole knew
her mother had found it easier to relate to the easy-
going Molly than to her obstinate older daughter.

It was understandable. Her mother had been
more like Molly. Nicole would bet money Lori had
been a strong-willed child. That's why Lori could
appreciate someone with ''spunk.''

The more she thought about it, the more Nicole

decided she'd misjudged the nanny. She should give Lori another chance. After all, Nicole might be obstinate, but she was also open-minded. And this time she was willing to admit she just might have made a mistake.

It had been less than a month since Molly first spoke and Lori couldn't believe the change. Within a week, Molly had started putting sentences together. Now it was hard to believe she'd ever been silent.

Although her words were sometimes halting, this morning Molly had chatted like a little magpie, talking about the friends she hoped would be in her class and the new teacher that she would have this year.

"I'm sure Ms. Anderson will be very nice," Lori said, hoping her words would prove true.

"Will you walk me to the room?" Molly cast Lori an imploring look as they turned into the school's parking lot.

Lori pulled into an open space and turned off the engine. "Is it okay?"

"Sure." Molly flung the door open and reached for her backpack. "All the mothers do it."

A tight band gripped Lori's chest making it difficult for her to breathe.

All the mothers do it.

Molly had said the words matter-of-factly, almost as if Lori *were* her mother and not just her nanny. Lori shook the silly thought aside and stepped out of the car, suddenly reluctant to take on a role that wasn't her due. "Molly—"

"C'mon." Molly shifted her backpack from one hand to the other, her gaze focused on the school's front door. "They're starting to go in."

Still hesitant, Lori glanced toward the crowd being herded through the huge double doors, noticing for the first time all the women walking among the children. Surely not all of them were mothers.

"Okay," Lori said finally, "I'll walk you to your classroom."

Molly grabbed Lori's hand and pulled her across the parking lot and into the building. Though the three-story structure was old, the floors were polished to a mirror finish and the walls had been freshly painted.

A small boy raced by, knocking Lori into a young woman with short brown hair.

"I'm sorry," Lori said.

"Don't be." The woman smiled. "Being jostled in the crowd makes me feel like *I'm* back in school again."

Lori smiled. "I was just thinking the same thing."

"I'm Anne Conard." The woman extended her hand and Lori shook it, introducing herself.

"Is your daughter new to Thomas Jefferson?"

the woman asked, glancing at Molly. "I don't think I've seen you around."

"Molly's been going here since kindergarten," Lori said. "And I'm not her mother. I'm her nanny."

"That's too bad." Anne made no attempt to hide her disappointment. "I was hoping to recruit you for our parent council."

"If it's not just for mothers, I could ask Mr. McCashlin if he'd be interested."

"Andrew McCashlin?" Anne lifted a brow.

"That's right," Lori said. "Do you know him?"

"Not him." Anne shook her head. "But my younger brother Todd was a friend of his son, Clay."

"I know Clay very well," Lori said. "In fact, he's married to my best friend."

"What a small world." Anne chuckled. Her gaze lingered on Lori. "I have to tell you I'm disappointed you aren't Molly's mother. It would have been a blast to have someone my age on the committee. A lot of the parents at this school are older."

Lori lifted a shoulder in a slight shrug and smiled. It *would* have been fun to get involved, but it wasn't her place. She was only the nanny, and no amount of wishing was going to change that fact.

* * *

"How was school today, Molly?" Drew took a helping of whipped potatoes and passed the serving dish to Lori.

"My teacher's name is Ms. Anderson," Molly said, stabbing a green bean with her fork. "She has two cats at home. Can we have a cat?"

Drew had to smile. He wondered if he'd ever get tired of hearing the sound of his daughter's voice. "You're allergic to cats, remember?"

A tiny frown marred Molly's brow. "I forgot. Maybe we can get a rat. We have a rat in our classroom."

Drew just smiled and shifted his gaze to Nicole. He'd learned long ago the wisdom of silence in dealing with such requests. "And how was your day?"

Nicole took a tablespoonful of potatoes and placed the dish on the table. "School was...school. But cheerleading practice went great. The girls really liked this cool new move I taught them."

Rats? Cheerleading? Drew wondered when the education system had been reduced to rodents and pom-pom routines.

"A new cheerleading move." Drew nodded as if he understood. Actually he was way out of his element. But he figured he couldn't go wrong if he stuck to basic questions. "Did you make it up?"

A peel of laughter greeted his words. "Dad-dy, of course I didn't make it up."

He tilted his head. "If you didn't make it up, where *did* it come from? Don't tell me it just dropped from the sky."

Nicole giggled. She cast a quick sideways glance to her left. "Lori taught it to me."

Drew's gaze shot to Lori, who glanced up from cutting her meat and gave him a little smile. He didn't know what surprised him more—that Nicole would listen to anything Lori said or that Lori would know some move Nicole considered cool. "You're into cool cheerleading moves?"

The words must have sounded as awkward on his tongue as they felt because both Lori and Nicole smiled.

"Our squad in high school went to nationals every year," Lori said. "The move I taught Nicole got us first place in our division my senior year."

"It's really hard," Nicole admitted. "But Lori said if the girls want to come over here sometime, she'd help us."

"She did, did she?" Drew's gaze shifted from Nicole to Lori. Though she hid it well, he could see the satisfied gleam in Lori's eye.

The wall that had stood between Lori and his oldest daughter had started to crumble.

Drew didn't know why. Or how. He only knew he couldn't be more pleased.

Chapter Sixteen

American Teen

Dear Lorelei Love,
Last week on impulse I colored my hair red. It was that fantastic new shade that you see in all the magazines and I was sure I was going to look great. Unfortunately I was wrong. I ended up looking like a cross between *I Love Lucy* and Bozo the Clown. I could understand the other kids at school laughing, but my best friend laughed right along with them. She apologized later, but now I'm not sure I want to be her friend.

                         Fickle Farrah's Friend in Fresno

Dear Farrah's Friend,
I hate to hear those bad-hair stories. It reminds me of the time I darkened my hair and looked like I should be reciting incantations over a bubbling cauldron. Seriously, when good hair goes bad it can be devastating. But the only way to get through it is to laugh it off· and find a good hairdresser ASAP! I agree that it was wrong for your friend to laugh. But to scrap a friendship over such an incident, especially after she apologized seems a bit extreme. Give yourself a little time to cool off and I think you'll agree that forgiveness is the best approach.

                         LL

"**Y**our daughter is a delight to have in class, Mr. McCashlin." Ms. Anderson, Molly's third-grade teacher, sat back in her desk chair and smiled at Drew.

Drew released the breath he'd been holding. When Mrs. Graham had told him that Molly's teacher had called and wanted to meet with him, he'd been surprised. And more than a little concerned. After all, parent-teacher conferences were less than two weeks away. Why would Molly's teacher insist on meeting with him now?

"Glad to hear it," Drew said. "But surely that wasn't the reason you called this conference?"

Ms. Anderson flushed. Her gaze shifted to her

desk and she busily straightened a stack of papers before looking up to meet his gaze.

"This is extremely awkward," the teacher said at last. "And if it's none of my business, just say so...."

Drew frowned. Something was obviously bothering the young teacher. But what could it be? Molly loved school and Ms. Anderson had just said she was a delight....

"Are you and your wife having marital troubles?" The question tumbled out of the teacher's mouth.

Drew's head jerked up. "Marital troubles?"

A splash of pink colored the teacher's pale cheeks. She nodded.

His brows drew together. Although Ms. Anderson was new to the school this year, Molly's records should have indicated her mother was deceased.

"I wasn't sure if I should mention it." The teacher's blush deepened. "But I talked with the school counselor and she felt in view of Molly's obvious distress...."

"What distress?" Drew's voice rose. "No one has said anything before about any distress."

Ms. Anderson's eyes widened at the abrupt tone. She started to speak, then clamped her mouth shut and pulled a picture out from a top desk drawer and handed it to Drew. "This pretty much says it all."

Hoping for an answer, Drew took the picture and studied it. Though the piece of art was crudely drawn in crayon, it was clearly their home in the background. A male sticklike figure with short brown hair stood in front of the house with two girls, one on each side. The taller girl had long dark hair and he pegged her as Nicole, which left the short blonde as Molly. Way off to the right side, almost off the page, stood a tall blond-haired female.

Lori?

"We asked the children to draw a picture of their family," Ms. Anderson said in a gentle tone. "This is what your daughter drew. When I asked Molly why she'd put her mommy way over to the side like that, she started to cry."

Drew stared at the picture, a sudden tightness gripping his chest. "Molly's mother died in a car accident two years ago."

"Oh, my goodness." Regret splashed across the young teacher's face. "I didn't know."

"I'm surprised the counselor didn't tell you," Drew said, handing the picture back to the teacher.

"She's new this year, too," Ms. Anderson said. "And I know she hasn't had a chance to go through all the files yet."

"In the future, that might be a good place to

look first,'' Drew said. ''Karen died when Molly was in kindergarten. That information would have been in her file.''

''A blond-haired woman brought Molly to school that first day,'' Ms. Anderson pointed out. ''They looked so much alike, I just thought—''

''That was Molly's nanny,'' Drew said.

''I really got this mixed-up, didn't I?'' The teacher gave a nervous laugh, clearly embarrassed. ''It's just that when I tried to comfort Molly, and she kept saying 'I don't want her to go,' I assumed she meant her mother. It sounded like her fears concerned something that was happening now. I'm so sorry.''

''I know you were only trying to help Molly,'' Drew said. ''I appreciate your concern.''

''She must have loved her mother very much.''

Drew nodded. ''They were very close.''

But even as he reassured Ms. Anderson, Drew wondered what the teacher would say if she knew that his wife's hair had been dark, not blond.

Drew leaned back in the kitchen chair, hoping he was making the right decision. His talk with Molly's teacher had disturbed him more than he'd let on. He'd mulled the discussion over in his head for a few days before deciding to discuss the situation with Lori.

He'd told her only that they needed to talk and

she'd agreed to meet him in the kitchen after Molly was in bed. Once she'd sat down, he'd quickly filled her in on what had happened at the school.

"What do you want me to do?" Lori said softly, her eyes filled with genuine concern. Though she'd changed into running pants and a long-sleeved T-shirt, and her hair was pulled back into a loose braid, Drew thought she looked beautiful.

Drew chose his words carefully. "I think it would help if you could reassure her that you'll always be a part of her life. That might lessen her fear of losing you."

Lori stared at her hot cocoa for a long moment. She dipped a spoon into the steaming chocolate and stirred the marshmallows with the tip, her expression pensive.

"I'm afraid I can't do that," she said at last.

Drew set his cup on the table with a slow controlled movement. "Why not?"

"Because—" Lori took a deep breath "—I *won't* always be part of Molly's life. And promising something I can't deliver will only hurt her more."

Drew's gut tightened, but when he spoke, his tone gave no indication of his inner turmoil. "Why can't you? Always be a part of her life, I mean."

He couldn't believe she was still considering leaving. Despite keeping their distance physically, in the past few weeks he and Lori had grown so close, he couldn't imagine life without her. And he'd started to think she felt the same.

Every Sunday after church, they'd all discuss the sermon in the car on the way home. Although Drew had initiated the conversation originally as a way to spur discussion, the talks had been unexpectedly therapeutic. After a sermon on forgiveness, when Nicole had vented her anger over her mother's death and the drunk driver's light sentence, Drew had been able to share his own feelings for the first time since the accident.

He has also made it a point at the dinner table to bring up topics that they could all discuss. And in the process, he not only learned how Lori felt about different issues, but what was going on in his daughters' heads, as well.

But that didn't help him now. He didn't have a clue what she was thinking.

"...because I'm not going to be working here forever," Lori said. "My employment contract is short-term, remember?"

He realized with a start that while his mind had been wandering, Lori had continued talking. But it was the opening Drew had been waiting for, the chance to convince Lori she belonged here. With him. With the girls. Even if she wasn't in love with him yet, there was no reason she had to leave at the end of December.

"I'll be glad to extend your contract," he said. "With a generous raise."

"Thanks," Lori said. "But no thanks."

Could it be she actually meant to leave? For the first time Drew realized he might actually lose this woman. She sounded so sure, so determined. Like her mind was already made up. He leaned forward, his blood running cold. "Don't you *want* to stay?"

"Oh, Drew." Lori expelled a heavy sigh. "This isn't about me *wanting* to stay. It's about me needing to move on with my life."

She was looking at him expectantly and Drew forced himself to nod as if he understood. But he didn't understand, not at all. He knew he wasn't the kind of man she was looking for, but he believed, given time, she'd change her mind. Just like he'd changed his.

It hadn't taken him long to realize that Lori's physical attributes were just a small part of who Lori was as a person.

Her kindness to Nicole, despite his daughter's often antagonistic attitude. Her loving concern toward Molly. The respect she showed Mrs. Graham. How could he not love her?

He'd fallen for her from the very beginning. He just hadn't wanted to admit it. To her. Or to himself. But now there was no denying the fact. And he could scarcely believe that he, who'd never been on the losing end of a business deal, stood on the verge of losing something far more important.

"You know," Lori continued, the slight smile on her lips seeming to mock the seriousness of their discussion, "that in time you'll marry. And then where will I be? Out of a job, that's where."

"That'll never happen," Drew answered confidently, knowing the only woman he wanted to marry was the one sitting in front of him.

"Whether you want to admit it or not, it will happen and it will be a problem." Lori pushed aside her cup and leaned forward, her arms resting on the table. "That's why it's best if we stick to our original plan."

"But plans change." Drew spoke lightly as if what they were discussing was of no more consequence than last night's dinner menu instead of something that had the potential to tear his world apart. "Why can't you stay longer?"

"Because I have my own life to live," Lori said, meeting his gaze. The firm resolve in her eyes drove any thought of declaring his love from his mind.

"What about Molly?" Drew asked, hating himself for dragging his daughter into this discussion. "Where does this leave her?"

"I've started preparing her for the fact that after Christmas I'll be gone," Lori said, her gaze shifting over his shoulder, her hands folded tightly together on the table before her. "You can help by never giving her the impression I might stay. Because we both know that's not going to happen.''

"You *could* change your mind,'' Drew said, holding on to one last hope.

"I won't.'' Lori shook her head. "I'll be leaving at the end of December, and there's nothing you can do or say that will make me stay.''

"I don't want you to go.'' Molly lifted her gaze from her dollhouse, her big eyes glistening with tears.

"I know you don't, kiddo.'' Lori drew a ragged breath. She'd known it wouldn't be easy, but she'd never thought it would be this hard. Over the past few weeks, each time Lori had tried to talk to Molly about her plans, the little girl had withdrawn into silence.

At least this time Molly had talked.

It would be so easy to take the little girl in her arms and tell her she'd changed her mind. Drew would be ecstatic. Though she was scheduled to leave in less than two months, Lori knew he hadn't even begun to look for a replacement. She hadn't been any more proactive. Only recently had she started apartment hunting, and so far she'd come up empty.

But staying would be the selfish thing to do. It would only prolong what would eventually happen anyway.

For the first few weeks after their talk about the future, Lori had continued to hope Drew would come to love her as much as she loved him. After all, they got along so well. They enjoyed the same activities, and for all Drew's talk of their age difference, she hadn't noticed it being a factor at all. They'd had fun. They'd laughed. But it wasn't enough.

Lori wanted more. She wanted him to hold her hand and touch her cheek. She wanted him to love her. And she couldn't live like this much longer. If she didn't get out of here soon, she just might go crazy one day and beg Drew McCashlin to love her, and really embarrass them both.

"I want you to know that no matter where I am—" Lori knelt down next to Molly and put her arms around the little girl "—I will always love you."

"I wish you were my mommy." Molly wrapped her arms around Lori's neck.

"I wish I were, too," Lori whispered against the girl's silky hair, her heart aching. She'd spent years praying for God to send her a man without children. Now she'd give anything to marry the man she loved and be a mother to his girls.

Molly pulled herself back from Lori's arms and stared, her blue eyes unflinching and direct. "Is it because you don't love my daddy? Is that why you can't be my mommy?"

All she had to do was say yes, that although her daddy was a wonderful man, she wasn't in love with him. But the words stuck in Lori's throat. "I-I—"

Molly gazed up at her. The innocence and trust in her eyes made it impossible for Lori to lie.

"I do love him, pumpkin." Lori swallowed hard against the lump in her throat. "He just doesn't love *me*."

A frown marred Molly's brow. "But why?"

"I don't know, honey," Lori said. "I wish I did."

Nicole stepped back from the doorway before Lori or Molly could notice her. She scampered down the hall and pulled her bedroom door shut behind her, Lori's words echoing in her head.

I do love him. He just doesn't love me.

The sincerity in the woman's tone was evident. Hearing Lori's words to Molly only confirmed what Nicole had already come to believe: she'd been wrong in ever thinking that Lori was after her father for his money. Wrong in thinking Lori would sleep with her dad without being married to him. Wrong in thinking Lori didn't care about her and Molly.

Guilt sluiced through her at the thought of how she'd trashed Lori to her dad. That had been a mistake. A big one. Now Nicole had to figure out a way to make it right. For all their sakes.

Chapter Seventeen

American Teen

Dear Lorelei Love,
Several months ago, out of the blue, my boyfriend told me he just wanted us to be friends. I acted like I didn't care and told him I felt the same. But I didn't feel the same. I loved him with my whole heart. Now he says he's changed his mind and he loves me, too. He wants me to accept his fraternity pin. Am I a fool to give him a second chance?

Uncertain in Unadilla

Dear Uncertain,
The only foolish thing would be to let the love of your life slip through your fingers.

Not all of us get even a first chance at love,
so if you love him and he loves you, I say
go for it. And I wish you only the best!

LL

Lori bounded down the stairs, energized by the
thought of having the whole day to herself. With
Nicole at cheerleading camp and Molly at her
grandmother's house, there was nothing tugging at
her time. She'd even finished this month's column
for *American Teen* ahead of schedule.

Even the weather had cooperated and given her
a bright Indian summer day. A day made for in-
line skating. For a brief moment Lori wished Kaitlyn were in town. It would have been fun to Rol-
lerblade along the lake with a friend at her side,
talking and maybe stopping for lunch at that little
trailside café.

But she'd never had a problem entertaining herself and today would be no exception. Lori stopped
at the bottom of the back stairs and stretched. Once
she'd finished, she opened the closet door and
pulled out her skates.

Hugging the blades to her chest, she headed for
the kitchen. With the day projected to be in the
low eighties, the one thing she couldn't afford to
forget was her water bottle.

Lori pushed open the kitchen door then skidded
to an abrupt stop. ''What are you doing home?''

Drew laughed and raised his coffee cup in a mock salute. "Good morning to you, too."

"G-good morning," Lori stammered. Drew was the last person she'd thought would still be home at ten o'clock on a Saturday morning. The way he'd talked the other night about his workload, she'd expected him to be out of the house at six. After all, the girls were gone and there was no reason for him to be hanging around home.

Unless he didn't feel well....

Lori narrowed her gaze. To her scrutinizing eye he didn't look sick. In fact, he looked incredible.

Dressed in khaki shorts and a royal blue polo, the man looked more ready for a day of relaxation than a day in the office. Her gaze rose to his face. To the square jaw and the full lips.

Her heart picked up speed remembering the sweet feel of that mouth against hers. It had been six long frustrating weeks since they'd decided to keep things strictly business.

He'd kept his word, but sometimes she'd catch him staring at her with such naked longing, it would take her breath away. It took all her willpower at such times not to reach out to him.

There was no doubt in her mind that, regardless of all his talk about keeping their distance, Drew would respond to such an overture. He was, after all, a man. And the electricity that had been there since the moment they'd first met still hung in the air whenever they were together.

But though the thought of kissing him sent a flash of heat up her spine, Lori knew settling for mere physical pleasure would be shortchanging them both.

She wanted him to love her, not just desire her. She wanted to be his wife and the mother of his children. She wanted it all. And she refused to settle for less.

"Going in-line skating?" Drew's amused voice pulled her from her reverie.

Horrified, Lori realized she'd been standing there staring at his lips!

Heat rose up her neck, but she forced a casual tone. "How'd you know?"

That incredible dimple flashed in his left cheek. "The fact that you're holding those skates was my first clue."

His eyes danced with good-natured humor and when he chuckled, Lori couldn't help but laugh right along with him.

She plopped down into the chair next to him and set the skates on the floor. "What are you doing home today?"

"Relaxing," he said. "Enjoying the view."

He smiled, his gaze lazily appraising the shorts that had been just the right length upstairs but now felt too short, moving to the tiny T-shirt that covered more of her than a swimsuit top ever would but suddenly seemed too scanty.

Lori rose, her heart skittering in her chest.

"I'm just going to get my water bottle and head out," she said. "The day's too beautiful to waste."

She could feel Drew's gaze follow her as she moved to the refrigerator and opened the door.

"Is Tom going with you?"

"Tom?" Lori turned one hand on the open refrigerator door, the other clutching a bottle of mineral water. "Why would Tom be going with me?"

Drew shrugged. "You two were friends...."

"I haven't seen Tom in months," Lori said. "Knowing him, I'm sure he's got a new girlfriend by now."

Drew's gaze never left her face. "Does that bother you?"

"Not at all," Lori answered truthfully.

"That seems odd."

"Why?" Lori said, raising a brow. "Do you miss Susan?"

Drew stared for a moment before answering.

"No. Not at all."

"There you have it," Lori said.

"Have what?"

"Your answer," she said. "Everyone knows you only miss someone you care about."

Drew's Rollerblades had been a birthday gift last year from Nicole. Though he wasn't sure he'd ever use them, he and Nicole had skated along the lake-front a couple of times. And once he got the hang of it, he'd discovered he enjoyed the activity.

Like now.

A beautiful woman. A beautiful day. It didn't get much better than this. Drew glanced sideways at Lori skating effortlessly down the wide concrete walk.

When Nicole had warned him that Lori had been seriously looking at apartments, Drew knew the time for waiting was over. He'd had Celia invite Molly over for the day and Nicole came up with some excuse about cheerleading camp in order to give Lori and him some time alone.

"Having fun?" Lori's voice broke into his thoughts.

He flashed Lori a smile and took her hand, pulling her over to a stone wall alongside the path. "Let's sit for a few minutes."

"Don't tell me you're getting tired already," she said in a teasing tone.

"I am tired," Drew admitted, suddenly realizing just how much he meant those words. He was tired of all the subterfuge, of the game playing, of pretending to not care. "We can't go on like this."

Lori's smile wavered and disappointment filled her voice. "We can go back if you want."

He took her hands and held them loosely in his, the warmth of her flesh reassuring.

"I don't want to go back." He stared out over the waters of Lake Michigan and realized it was the truth. He had survived a profound loss, but he *had* survived. And now it was time to move on. Time to start living again. Time to give himself permission to love again. "I want to go forward."

Lori's brow furrowed. She tilted her head. "I'm afraid I don't understand."

Drew took a deep breath and plunged ahead. "From the moment you came to live with us, I was attracted to you. At first I was embarrassed by my feelings. I mean, you're a friend of my son's."

"Drew, don't—"

"Lori, please just listen. What I have to say won't take long." He smiled and was reassured when she smiled back. "I found I enjoyed spending time with you. And I really liked kissing you. But things moved along so fast. I knew I wasn't what you were looking for."

"I never said—"

"You said you wanted to have fun and that you didn't want to settle down for a long time."

"You told your mother-in-law that we were just friends."

Drew didn't remember Lori being there for that part of the conversation, but it hardly mattered now.

"Back then I didn't know what I was feeling," he said. "But I know what I'm feeling now."

"And what is that?" Her voice was soft and low and the world around him ceased to exist.

He brought her fingers to his lips. "I love you, Lori. I want to marry you and spend the rest of my life making you happy."

The smile that broke across her face was brighter than the overhead sun. She wrinkled her nose. "Are you sure you don't think of me as just a friend?"

"A friend?" Drew pulled her to him and met her gaze. "You *are* my friend. But I want you to be so much more. I want you to be my wife, my lover, the mother of my children. I want it all."

"So do I," she said.

"You do?"

Lori nodded.

"I can't believe it," he said, his voice filled with wonder. "We're going to be married."

"About that," Lori said. "There's only one problem—"

"Problem?" Drew shook his head and brushed her lips with his. "You love me. I love you. The only problem we have is figuring out how soon we can pull together a wedding."

Molly sat on Nicole's bed, her legs folded beneath her. "Daddy asked Lori to marry him."

"Shut up." Nicole dropped her hairbrush to the dressing table with a clatter. Her father had told her he was going to ask Lori to marry him, but she wondered if he'd chicken out at the last minute. "He did not."

"Did, too," Molly said. "I heard 'em talking downstairs."

Nicole moved to the bed and plopped down next to her sister, excitement coursing through her veins. "Tell me what he said."

Molly thought for a moment. "He said, 'C'mon, Lorelei Love, don't be so stubborn. Say you'll marry me.'"

"Lorelei Love?" Nicole sat up straight. "Why would he call her that?"

"I imagine because that's her name," Mrs. Graham said from the bathroom doorway and Nicole realized with a start that the housekeeper was still in the room, putting away linens. "Or at least it's the name she uses for that column."

"Column?" Nicole asked.

"For that teenager magazine," Mrs. Graham said. "Not that I've read it or anything."

Nicole's mouth dropped open. Lori Loveland was Lorelei Love? Hot anger rose within her until Nicole realized her confidences were still safe. Lori had no way of knowing she was Mia. And if Nicole had her way, Lori never would find out. Nicole looked back at her sister. "What did Lori tell Dad?"

"She said no."

Nicole's head jerked up at the sound of her father's voice. He stood in the doorway with Lori at his side.

"I didn't say no," Lori said softly, looking up at him. "I said I wanted to discuss it with you girls first."

Her father's gaze met Nicole's. She knew what he wanted her to say. But Nicole also knew from the look on Lori's face that complete and total honesty was the only answer she'd accept.

Nicole paused, remembering how alone she'd felt after her mother died. Since Lori had arrived, the house hadn't seemed nearly so empty. The light was back in her father's eye and Molly now laughed and talked like any other seven-year-old.

"Nicole, I want to make one thing clear. If I do marry your father I want you to know I'm not going to try to take your mother's place. But I would like to be your friend. And, if I ever can be of any help, or give you any advice—"

"Like the kind of advice you give in your column?" Nicole lifted a brow.

"Nicole," Drew growled a warning.

"It's okay." Lori placed a hand on his sleeve. Her gaze shifted to Nicole. "Lori or Lorelei, the advice would be the same."

Though Lori appeared perfectly calm, Nicole could hear the tension in her voice. And when Lori glanced at her father for reassurance, his hand slipped around her waist.

Nicole sighed. Despite her cynicism, she'd always been a sucker for true love. She met Lori's gaze. "If some thirty-year-old chick wrote to you and said the guy she was madly in love with had proposed—what would you tell her?"

An odd look flickered across Lori's face. "First I'd have to know if there were any obstacles—"

"Let's say there weren't any," Nicole said.

The tension in Lori's face eased. "Then I'd tell her if she loved him, she should say yes."

"That's your answer then," Nicole said. "Just follow your own advice."

"Nicole…" Her father frowned and Nicole could tell he'd missed the whole point.

But the broad smile on Lori's face told Nicole that Lori had her answer.

"Drew." Lori turned and lifted her face to him. "Is your offer still good?"

"Of course it is," he said without hesitation. "I love you. I want to marry you."

"Then let's do it." Lori raised her arms and placed them around his neck.

A look of wonder filled his eyes. "You're really saying yes?"

Nicole rolled her eyes. For someone so smart in

business, her dad could be incredibly stupid when it came to women. It was a miracle he'd found someone as great as Lorelei Love.

Lori met Nicole's gaze and she gave the girl a quick wink before her gaze returned to Drew.

"I'll be your wife," Lori said. "And I'll love you forever."

"I always knew we were on the same wavelength." Drew wrapped his arms around Lori and pulled her close.

Molly jumped up and down. "Yippee. Daddy and Lori are getting married."

Nicole felt like cheering herself. Instead she took her little sister by the hand and gave her dad the greatest gift she could give him at the moment—some time alone with the woman he loved.

"You're telling me your nanny is Lorelei Love?" Erin shook her head in disbelief. "No way."

"Way," Nicole said. It was still hard for her to believe. "The funny thing is, she and I were e-mailing each other for months and I never had a clue we were living right under the same roof."

"So what'd she say when she found out?" Erin looked up from the toenail she was painting. "Did she totally freak?"

"I didn't tell her," Nicole said. "She has no idea that I'm Mia."

"Mia?" Erin wrinkled her nose.

"That was the name I used." Nicole smiled. "What's the matter? Don't you like it?"

Erin ignored the question. "Why haven't you told her?"

Moving to the window, Nicole pushed back the draperies and stared out. "I told Lorelei Love *all* my feelings—we wrote about practically everything. Would you want your mother to know every thought you ever had?"

"No." Erin finished painting her last toenail and carefully capped the bottle. "But she's not your mom. Even after she marries your dad she'll still just be your stepmom."

Molly had already asked Lori if she could call her Mommy. Lori had told them they could call her whatever they liked, and whatever they decided was okay with her.

It was another example of Lori's generous nature and it only made Nicole feel worse about all the bad things she'd said in the past.

"Did I tell you I bought them a wedding gift?" Nicole asked, changing the subject.

"You did? Why?" Erin frowned. "I mean, it's not like they need anything."

"I know," Nicole said. "But I'm happy they're getting married and I wanted them to know it. That's why I picked out something they can both enjoy."

"My mother gave my uncle and his new wife a set of knives," Erin said with a shrug. "She said that's a gift they can both enjoy for years."

Nicole smiled, imagining her father's reaction when he opened *her* gift. Somehow she had the feeling he and Lori would enjoy her gift a lot more then a set of knives.

In fact, she'd bet on it.

Epilogue

American Teen

Dear Readers,
In lieu of my column this month, *American Teen* will be rerunning the top twelve questions/answers from the past year. For most of us, this year has been one of change. And I'm no exception. I started out this year enjoying the single life and I will be closing it out as a new bride. Yes, it's true, Lorelei Love is tying the knot this month. It's an exciting time in my life, but also a little scary. But I know it's the right move because I love the man I'm marrying, and he loves me. It just doesn't get much better than that!

Wishing you all only the best during this holiday season and I'll see you next year.

LL

Lori flopped on the soft bed and heaved a contented sigh. It had been a beautiful day and a perfect wedding. They'd been surrounded by friends and family. Clay had been Drew's best man, while his wife, Kaitlyn, had been her maid of honor. Nicole had been resplendent in her bridesmaid dress and Molly had looked like a fairy princess scattering flowers down the church aisle.

But it had been God's presence that had meant the most. When Lori had stood in His house and said those sacred vows, God had been there beside her, whispering that this was what He'd planned for her all along.

Lori sat up and smiled at her new husband. "We did it. Can you believe it? We really did it."

Drew turned, a wicked gleam in his eye. "No," he said. "We haven't done it. But we will soon enough."

He pulled off his jacket, tossing it onto a nearby chair.

Lori's heart skittered in her chest and languid warmth filled her limbs. She patted the bed. "Why don't you come over here and put some action behind those words, Mr. McCashlin?"

Drew grinned and unfastened his cummerbund. "I intend to do just that, Mrs. McCashlin."

The black sash flew across the room and landed on a side table atop a neatly wrapped package.

Lori widened her gaze.

Drew moved toward her.

Jumping up from the bed, Lori eluded his outstretched arms. "Not yet."

Drew stopped and two lines of worry appeared between his brows. "Sweetheart, what's the matter?"

Lori headed straight to the package with the big white bow. She grabbed the gift and offered the present to her new husband.

Drew stared, but made no move to take it from her outstretched hand. "You want to open wedding gifts? Now?"

Lori had to laugh at the expression on his face. "Not all of them. Just this one."

When he hesitated, she laughed again. "C'mon, take it. It's from your daughter. Nicole made me promise you'd open it as soon as we got to the hotel."

"Later." Drew's hand reached for her. "I can think of a few other things I'd rather be doing right about now."

Though Lori wanted nothing more than to toss the package aside and fall into his arms, she playfully slapped his hand away. "I promised. Please, just open it."

With a resigned sigh Drew took it from her. He

yanked off the bow, ripping the paper with his other hand. The pink and white box gave him pause for only a second. He shrugged and peeled it open.

"What the…" Drew stared, amazed. Nestled in the tissue paper was the black lace nightie with a matching thong he'd seen in the Victoria's Secret window at the mall. "Nicole saw me admiring one just like this, months ago."

"It's lovely." Lori leaned over his shoulder. "But are you sure it's your size? That thong looks a little small." She shot him an impish smile and then had to laugh at his expression. "Seriously, let me see it."

He held out the tiny scraps of fabric to her, his blue eyes suddenly as dark as the ocean floor.

Lori's pulse quickened and her knees went weak. She pretended to study the garment. "You know, it looks more my size than yours."

"You forget," he said. "This is my gift. She gave it to me."

Lori pretended to pout. "So you're not going to share?"

Drew's lips twitched. "I'm a fair man. I think you'll find I'm willing to compromise."

Lori grinned. "This sounds interesting. Please continue."

"Isn't it obvious?" His smile widened and he

leaned forward and kissed her nose. "*You* put it on. *I* take it off."

The very thought sent Lori's blood coursing through her body like an awakened river.

"Sounds like a fair deal." Lori reached forward and kissed him full on the lips, gently taking the nightie from his hands.

For the briefest of moments she gazed up at this man she adored, the man who was now her beloved husband. He was everything she'd ever wanted and everything she needed. And God had known it all along.

Sending a quick prayer of thanks heavenward, Lori reached for the buttons on her dress, eagerly anticipating this night and all the nights to come.

*   *   *   *   *

*Be sure to look for
Cynthia Rutledge's next story,
Loving Grace,
in a special 2-in-1 collection
THE HARVEST
by Cynthia Rutledge
and Gail Gaymer Martin
Available October 2003
wherever Love Inspired books are sold.*

Dear Reader,

Lori and Drew were first introduced in my March 2003 Silhouette Romance novel, *Kiss Me, Kaitlyn*. When writing that book, I had no plans to bring any secondary characters back for a book of their own. But Lori and Drew were such interesting characters that when the book was completed I found I couldn't let them go!

If you're interested in finding out more about Drew's son, Clay, and his romance with Lori's best friend Kaitlyn, I encourage you to pick up a copy of *Kiss Me, Kaitlyn*. It's a cute story that I'm sure you'll enjoy.

All my best,

Cynthia Rutledge

Love Inspired

HEAVEN KNOWS

BY JILLIAN HART

John Corey's soul ached for his late wife but he tried
to move forward as best he could for their beloved
little girl's sake. Like a gift from God, drifter
Alexandra Sims wandered into their lives and
turned it around. Suddenly, John began to believe
in love again, but would Alexandra's painful secret
stand in the way of true happiness?

Don't miss

HEAVEN KNOWS
On sale June 2003

Available at your favorite retail outlet.

Visit us at www.steeplehill.com

LIHK

Love Inspired™®

HART'S HARBOR

BY

DEB KASTNER

Dr. Kyle Hart had come to Safe Harbor to find peace. But the town matchmakers had other plans for the dashing widower. So when Kyle and the spontaneous Gracie Adams masqueraded as an engaged couple to outwit the matchmakers at their own game, he found himself finding love and healing where he least expected it....

Don't miss
HART'S HARBOR
the third installment of
SAFE HARBOR
The town where everyone finds shelter from the storm!

On sale May 2003
Available at your favorite retail outlet.

Take 2 inspirational love stories FREE!

PLUS get a FREE surprise gift!

Mail to Steeple Hill Reader Service™

In U.S.
3010 Walden Ave.
P.O. Box 1867
Buffalo, NY 14240-1867

In Canada
P.O. Box 609
Fort Erie, Ontario
L2A 5X3

YES! Please send me 2 free Love Inspired® novels and my free surprise gift. After receiving them, if I don't wish to receive anymore, I can return the shipping statement marked cancel. If I don't cancel, I will receive 3 brand-new novels every month, before they're available in stores! Bill me at the low price of $3.99 each in the U.S. and $4.49 each in Canada, plus 25¢ shipping and handling and applicable sales tax, if any*. That's the complete price and a saving of over 10% off the cover prices—quite a bargain! I understand that accepting the books and gift places me under no obligation ever to buy any books. I can always return a shipment and cancel at any time. Even if I never buy another book from Steeple Hill, the 2 free books and the surprise gift are mine to keep forever.

103 IDN DNU6
303 IDN DNU7

Name	(PLEASE PRINT)	
Address	Apt. No.	
City	State/Prov.	Zip/Postal Code

* Terms and prices are subject to change without notice. Sales tax applicable in New York. Canadian residents will be charged applicable provincial taxes and GST. All orders subject to approval. Offer limited to one per household and not valid to current Love Inspired® subscribers.

INTLI_02

©1998 Steeple Hill

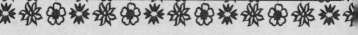

Love Inspired®

THE CARPENTER'S WIFE

BY

LENORA WORTH

No one wanted roots more than Rock Dempsey.
He finally met the woman he wanted to share his life
with in Ana Hanson. But nothing had ever come easy
for the woman he hoped to have and to hold forever.
Would it take some divine guidance from above
before she would become the carpenter's wife?

Don't miss
THE CARPENTER'S WIFE
On sale June 2003

*Available at your
favorite retail outlet.*